SELENE 3/8 - 3/14

Beth 3/14 - 3/17

Deb

Christa 3/23

Cathy 3/25

Chios 3/25 -

Christina 3/29 - 4/1/10

Priscilla - 4/1/10 - 4/3/10

Kevin 4/3 - 4/9

Lisa 4/9

HELP!
A Bear is
Eating Me!

Mykle Hansen

ERASERHEAD PRESS
PORTLAND, OREGON

ERASERHEAD PRESS

205 NE BRYANT
PORTLAND, OR 97211

WWW.ERASERHEADPRESS.COM

ISBN: 1-933929-69-3

The author would like to thank the
winter residents of Baja California for
their kind attention, and Karen Townsend
of Afterbirth Books for her assistance
with layout, proofreading and design.

This book is dedicated to bears everywhere.

1

You think *you* have problems? I'm being eaten by a
bear! Oh, but I'm sorry, forgive me, let's hear about *your*
problems. Mmm-hmm? So, your boss is mean to you? Is
your car not running well? Perhaps you're concerned about
the environment. Boo, hoo! Your environment just ate my
foot! I'm *bleeding* on your environment! And it's a small
consolation for the pain and the mess and the fear that I
would be feeling — were I not so well-prepared for adverse
excitement, were I not ingesting so many miraculous pain
killing drugs — a small consolation that I can now say
without fear of contradiction that MY PROBLEMS ARE
WORSE THAN YOURS. So just shut up about your
problems, okay? Okay.

If you were real, if you were here, and if you were a
decent person, I'm sure you would be right now summoning
HELP. Or maybe you'd be up a tree hiding from this bear,
but after this bear finally quit chewing on me and wandered
home, then you'd surely come down from your pansy perch
and check my vital signs, make sure that I'm okay, or at least
not dead yet, and upon finding me not-dead-yet you'd run
off to fetch a Forest Ranger, or an off-road ambulance, or
a Search & Rescue chopper with the range to reach us up
here in this stupid fancy Alaskan wilderness, carrying within
it a Rescue team to rescue me, and a Search team to find
this god damn black bear and shoot him in his god damn
black head! And also, ideally, some kind of off-road cargo

transport system, to tow my Rover back to the dealership in Anchorage, there to invoke the oh-so-costly and oh-so-worth-it All Disaster Coverage clause of my insurance, and get my poor lovely road machine repaired, polished, tuned and refueled for my triumphant recovery. And then the two of us — that is, me and my car — would drive off together into the Al-Can Highway sunset, never again to venture north of Vancouver.

Yeah, I love my car. I'm sure if you were here you'd ask me all about it: you'd want to know how well it handles (like butter on a steak), what kind of mileage it gets (rakishly poor!), and how much I paid for it (which would not be any of your fucking business — but lots, I assure you.). My car and I have spent a lot of quality time together this year: we've listened to my iPod through its five-point Surround Sound with Digital Bass Stiffening; slalomed across the expressways with its sure-footed Dynamic Traction Control; put the fear of man-meat into Marcia from Product Dialogue on its rear Oxford leather fold-back seat with Shiatsutronic Smart Massage; we've crept silently along the bike lanes like a shark by the shore, startling bicyclists with its thunderous horn before leaving them twitching in clouds of its viscous exhaust. But this is the first time — pinned as I am under its left rear independent axle, after the jack slipped and dropped the whole massive package on me, after I crawled under here for sanctuary, after the bear attacked me, after I started to change the inconceivably flat tire — this is my first bout of quality time *under* my car. Or, well, let's call it quantity time instead, because the actual quality is quite low. The top-end luxury appointments of my option package don't seem to extend to the bottom end. I'm telling you, it's not pretty down here. Foolish me, I kind of imagined that when I paid Javier's EZ-Clean twenty bucks to clean and detail my car, that Javier and his lazy illegal children cleaned and detailed *all* of it. But down here I see bolts and pipes and panels and wires caked in melted tundra, which I guess is part of the off-road aesthetic my car and I aspire to, but also covered in a thick black paté of urban road filth, and the mixture of the two is nicely rubbing off on my camel hair sport jacket, brand-new and now ruined. Plus — and this really would piss me off if I wasn't so very much Thinking Positive — plus something ... the radiator? The fibrillator? I don't know, I can't tell but *something* is very slowly dripping. A.K.A., releasing fluid. A.K.A, *leaking.* My powerful, virile and incredibly expensive car is less than a year old and already needs adult diapers. A car like this is not supposed to drip like that.

Plus that tire blowing out — ultimate cause of my current trauma ... Range Rover has a lot to answer for here, I think. And I'm sure somewhere there's a lawyer who agrees. That lawyer and I are going to make Range Rover pay my hospital bills once I get out of here, once I'm rescued, once this god damn bear quits alternating between chewing on my foot — *eeew* — and straining with the fat, stubby wolverine that is his arm to reach the rest of me here in this thankfully claustrophobic spot under the car. And he's eating not just my foot, mind you, but also my new Lands' End suede chukka boot: huntsman brown, size eleven and a half, left, two hundred eighty nine dollars, ninety five cents. This bear is costing me. This bear is going to pay.

Where is Edna? Where is that stupid woman, the woman I married? She's supposed to be here. Where are the useless little men of my department? Where's Marcia from Product Dialogue? How is it that after we all trek up

here with much fanfare, at great expense, for the purpose
of team-building, and a perfect team-building exercise like
this one presents itself, falls in my lap you could say … why
is my whole stupid team absent? Where are they? Back at
base camp, most likely; thumbs up butts, unable to motivate
their way out of a paper bag without me.

Note to self: fire team, divorce wife. Escape bear.

This is so not my fault! I'm not an idiot, you know.
I'm not naive in the ways of Bear. I researched them on the
Internet for *hours.*

Fact! American Black Bears such as this one grow to
between 130 and 500 pounds as adults — or larger, it would
appear — and are found in 32 states, including Alaska.
Fact! Black bears are solitary creatures, they forage for food
in clearings like this one, in forested regions such as here,
and they are omnivores, as we've seen. For their own safety
and as a team-building exercise I had the entire hunting
party memorize a set of bear facts and bear survival tips
before we came, and for my own amusement I brought a
bear-compatible shotgun, a Remington 870 police model
with Core-Lokt Ultra Bonded Sabot slugs, which is now
safely mounted above the driver's seat of the car I'm
trapped beneath, waiting to be fired bearwards by the first
lucky Search and Rescue operative to get off his ass and
make with some HELP!

It's utterly not my fault. I did everything right.
For instance: when I spied the bear, I did not run. Bears
can outrun people. That's a fact that I know. Instead I
stood tall, turned, faced the bear, shouted at the bear and
threw the tire wrench at the bear to let him know I was
A) a human, and B) not afraid. The bear in response
rose up upon his shaggy hind legs and tilted his head at
me, snuffling his nose and waving his paws around like a

stunned boxer. I took this to mean that he was getting a better look at and whiff of me, and that once he figured out he was dealing with Homo Sapiens — not just any Homo Sapiens, mind you, but MARV PUSHKIN, Senior Communications Creative, Corporate Warrior, Leader of Men, User of Women, Esquire subscriber — he would back off and return to his regularly scheduled bear lifestyle. That's Bear Survival Tip #1, by the way, from www.GoAlaska.com: Do not run away, but let the bear know who you are. (In retrospect, I realize I could have retreated into the Rover, but that would be showing weakness, which is deadly in the face of bears and definitely not Marv Pushkin's style.)

That was all going marvelously well until the bear sprinted up to me — who knew that much bear could move that fast? — and head-butted me backwards against the car. Then he began to sniff my pant legs, where I had recently spilled some smelly fluids and made a bit of a mess. I was dismayed and slightly embarrassed by this setback, but quick of wit and reflex. It was clearly time for www.GoAlaska.com's Bear Survival Tip #2: If the bear attacks, play dead. (The theory is, usually a bear only attacks because he's scared or threatened. Once he's decided you're not a threat he'll just pee on you and go home. Let me tell you, merely being peed on by a bear sees like a real luxury to me now.) So, I faked a heart attack and slumped over.

And then … he bit me! Unbelievable! And then he bit me again, and again … so I turned to Bear Survival Tip #3 … for what it was worth. Actually Tip #3 is pretty worthless, but here it is: If the bear continues to attack … fight back vigorously! Oh, thanks for that one, GoAlaska dot assholes! Never would have occurred to me. Maybe if

Tip #1 had been "Get in the Rover" and Tip #2 had been "Unlock the shotgun from the rack and load it with slugs" then Tip #3 would be a really handy, useful tip.

But wait … I think he's stopped. Oh joy. I can't hear much over the constant whir of mosquitoes, the opaque clouds of them that blot out the sun in this awful place … but I can hear that bear, breathing. He breathes like a congested linebacker hauling bricks up a staircase. He's just sitting there panting from the exertion of speed-eating, licking his paws, digesting my foot, thinking about what next to do with his bear evening. And the light is fading. As soon as he goes away I might manage to wriggle out from under this axle, or reach the jack and lift it off me, or even if I could just reach that cardboard Wally's box full of camping supplies — I stuck it under the car when I got the spare tire out, it's just a few inches beyond the reach of my left hand but if I could wriggle, without looking like food, without agitating the bear — then I could have a beer, because all this violence is making me thirsty.

If you were real, perhaps you'd be feeling some pity for me at this point. Well, save it. Of course it sucks, this being-eaten-by-a-bear experience, this mechanical failure, this whole vacation. But I'm a bright-side looker, a positive thinker. A winner. I'm trapped in a world of suck, yes, but one thing that doesn't suck is OxySufnix. And I'm going to take another one … in fact, I'll take two, because I've got lots. I'm sure you'd like to hear the lurid details of my agonizing, soul-searing pain, but honestly I couldn't tell you much about pain. I never feel it. All things considered, I feel great. I'm prepared, and double prepared, and over-prepared. My car let me down, my wife and my so-called team let me down, www.GoAlaska.com let me *way* the fuck down, but OxySufnix will not let me down. And if it does

I've also got Percoset, Vicadin and Prolexia right here in my breast-pocket pillbox, plus Antix, Ritalin, Mercantin, and a host of other unofficially prescribed favorites stowed away in the hollow end of my stash box, which resembles a small cartridge of wintermint Binaca. So fuck you, bear. Eat my foot, see if I care. I'll just settle in over here on the bright side, with my drugs, and wait you out.

Drugs are just one reason why I could never cast myself as one of those outdoor/nature/environment types. Technology treats me too well. Technology is so much better than nature at everything that nature's supposedly good at, I just don't see the point. Who needs scenery when you've got special effects? Who needs flora and fauna when you've got the Flora Channel and the Fauna Channel, not to mention the Woodland Park Zoo and a talented team of Latin-American landscapers delicately sculpting the front yard of your estate into a shapely oasis, year-round, pest-free? Who needs bracing wind and sea spray when you've got four independent climate control zones? Who needs a campfire when you've got a George Foreman Grill?

But the one thing I most adore about society, cities, the unnatural lifestyle in-toto, is this invention we've got called Justice. Have you heard of Justice, Mister Bear? Justice is awesome. Justice means that if you lived in Seattle and you walked up to me on the street and started rudely eating me in this way, without my explicit consent, my screams of pain and alarm would not go unheeded. In moments, a squad car would arrive on the scene and police officers would draw their weapons and order you to lay face down on the sidewalk. And if you refused to comply, then those officers — to protect their own lives! — would empty several rounds from their powerful human handguns into your ugly bear face, killing you into submission. Then a luxuriously appointed ambulance would arrive, and friendly paramedics would rush me to a nearby excellent hospital where on-call neurosurgeons would first extract my foot from the stomach of your still-warm carcass — your flesh twitching reflexively as they dig with their scalpels and saws — and then they would spend hours, if not days, fastidiously reattaching each severed nerve and tendon, stitching my foot back on my leg as if I were a torn teddy bear, only ever so much more important. Perhaps to reconstruct the gnarled bits of my ankle they would take a skin graft from my other leg, or from a donor leg, or maybe I'd even receive the first successful human foot transplant, a miracle of medical technology and anti-foot-rejection drugs. My miracle foot and I would be written up in medical journals and made briefly famous on local television, perhaps even asked to endorse products. Then later, when I could walk again, as well as before if not better, I'd buy a round of drinks for the nice policemen who introduced you to the exquisite human concept of Justice, and then I'd drive home resting upon soft new seat covers sewn from your stupid hide.

Certain people — hippies, I guess you'd call them — often insist to me that human beings *need* nature for some reason. Not just the nature we already have in our zoos and farms and parks, mind you, but also this wild, untended mess of Ur-Nature here in Alaska. We need this nature up here, they say, in order to survive down there, they say, and then they invoke all sorts of explanation about the interconnectedness of the spotted owls to the salmon to the cows to the lumber products, and sure, I'm not some trained environmentologist so I can't say they're totally wrong. Maybe they're right.

But this I do know: if human beings down in Seattle need for huge dangerous bears to be running around unchained in Alaska, then Alaska's going to have to address its Justice problem, posta la hasta. I mean, aren't there supposed to be Forest Rangers from Fish & Wildlife on patrol around here, making sure that people and animals obey the law and don't litter or double-park or eat each other without a permit? I haven't seen one ranger and I've been here for hours. Maybe, when they finally kick out those indigent Eskimos and start drilling some oil in this state, they'll get the income to import some tough inner city street cops to keep these bears in line. For that matter, if there was even one cell phone tower within five miles of here I could just dial 911! But there's not an ounce of reception on my Nokia picture-phone. No bars. This place is backwards and primitive and wrong.

It's dark, and the bear is quieting down. He's snuggled up against the side of the car, just a few feet from me. I think he's falling asleep. Maybe in a little while here I'll wriggle quietly free, and get the shotgun out of the Rover and offer Mister Bear some Remington 870 hollow-point after-dinner mints.

You think you're tough, Mister Bear? I've kicked bigger asses than yours. Eat, sleep and be hairy, for tomorrow you shall die.

2

I wasn't always being eaten by a bear. 24 hours ago I was stretched out on the self-inflating couch of Camp Image Team with a cold Bud in my hand, smelling the outdoor smells of our dainty forest clearing — some pleasant, others repulsive — and supervising the erection of a large six-man tent by the six small, erectionless men of my department. By supervising I mean offering them encouragement and gentle criticism as they wrestled incompetently with a complex umbrella-like nylon pod full of sticks and stakes and strings. That was me doing what I'm best at: delegating. I'm not the kind of manager who gets in his subordinates' way when they're busy, unless they're doing something wrong — and yeah, they usually are — but the thing is, the management wisdom is, you have to let them make those mistakes, and then gently rub their noses in it, for them to learn. And it's easier to delegate like that with a cold Bud in your hand.

And I would know all about that, because I'm sipping one right now! That's right! One cold, foamy cylinder of civilization's finest beer. I waited for my opening, I concentrated my will, made a superhuman effort and with one heroic lunge I grasped the cardboard box from Wally's Super Supply, dragged it over here and ripped it open to find: a hero's snacktime! There's Slim Jims, Bud, Bud Light (Edna's), Cliff Bars, Diet Pepsi (also Edna's), and I've barely scratched the surface. Man, there's something perfect about a Slim Jim and a cold Bud … even when it's cold outside, and you're cold, and something warm would be really nice. But a cold Bud has such powerful iconic cachet; it's telling every cell in my body that things are going to be just fine. It's telling my body The King Is Here, and This One's For Me. Now is the moment in my life when I must draw on my culture for strength.

I guess I've bled some. I haven't passed out or anything, at least not since the jack slipped and the car fell. All in all, I'm surviving. I've got my fluids, my meds, my snacks and my positive mental outlook. My prognosis is excellent. I could use some bug repellent, but whatever. A local crew of ants seems to want to lay claim to my hair, but whatever.

Image Team is going to find me. Or rather, Image Team is going to find some competent Search & Rescue professionals, who will then find me. Image Team couldn't find their own asses with a digital ass detector and a trail of breadcrumbs. But they ought to know how to delegate by now, isn't that what I've been trying to teach them? They've got Baumer's Toyota and their phones and a big-ass radio and it's only thirty miles of unpaved road to a paved road, and from there to a ranger station should be quick enough. They had better go get rangers. They had damn well better not wander out here looking for me on their own.

Of course, since this is supposed to be Team Building Weekend, they'll probably do exactly that, search for me on their own. Shit. I can totally see it: Frank Baumer will act all tough and give one of his gay motivational speeches from that book in the men's bathroom, like he always does when he's late on a project and has no ideas — which is usually — and then Halsey, always driven to kiss the largest ass he can smell, will suggest the group elect Baumer as an temporary leader, a sort of ersatz Me until the official Me can be found! And Wollencott and Frink, the Seattle Yes-Men's Chorus, will think that idea's a *peach*, an idea with *legs*, one they can *get behind*. And once they're done humping the legs of Halsey's gay peach, Baumer will give *another* fucking speech about big shoes to fill, footsteps of giants, not worthy, but okay, call me Boss if it makes you feel better. *(Note to self: fire Baumer.)* And then they'll unpack the little Motorola two-way radios I bought them, totally useless beyond one mile, and they'll fan out in all directions, calling my name and making noise and generally screaming HEY BEARS, COME AND EAT US. And then the bears will come and eat them. It'll serve them right for trying to be a team without me. Those guys are *nothing* without me.

If you existed and were here listening, you might ask just what sort of team-building exercise we had in mind, me and my department of trend-reversal morons, to travel so very far from our natural element, specifically our air-conditioned offices in the sleek twenty-second floor of Seattle's famous Merch building. What life-bending experience did we think this place could offer, to weld us together into a mighty unstoppable five-headed Godzilla of trend-reversal? Shit, I don't know, I don't believe in any of that teamwork bullshit. A team, really, is a group of people who do what I tell them to do, or else I fire them.

But basically we came to kill bears. Frink and Baumer apparently come up here every year to shoot ducks and fish and whatever else is small and defenseless and moves slowly and is halfway edible. And all those guys have been whining to me for some kind of off-site for months now, ever since I made the management error of letting one of our recalled hair product clients personally congratulate them for the supposedly excellent job they did following *my* orders and implementing *my* plan. Like that's not their job. The hair clients even gave us all little gift boxes full of — no kidding! — the self-same recalled hair product that we had just so deftly convinced the hair-washing public was safe and sexy and wouldn't cause excessive scabbing or patchy baldness. Right ... like I'm going to put that on my head. But the boys in Image Team did, and it did something to their brains — it made them think they deserved things.

So here's my whole doe-eyed, scabby-scalped department whining for an off-site, and then Frink and Baumer pitch this fishing, sniping, blowing duck calls and wearing orange underwear outside our pants in the beautiful Alaskan wilderness package. I immediately called them on their total lack of balls. I told them: boys, you are a pathetic pack of pussies if you need high-powered ammo to kill a *duck*. Ted Nugent uses a bow and arrow, for Christ's sake, and he kills moose and bears. Eats them, too. Raw! Drinks their blood! Subsists on nothing but moose burgers and bear sandwiches for months at a time, and then comes back home to NugeLand and writes deep, plaintive songs about the human condition. You little girls couldn't kill a moose if I sedated it, strapped it into an electric chair for you, showed you an instructional video and held your soft, trembling hands.

And of course they knew I was right. Being right is my job. The thing is, some managers hire people they're excited to work with. I prefer to hire people I'm excited to dominate. I don't want to work with my subordinates,

I want them to work *for* me, *instead of* me. I'm the idea man, and in marketing that's the only man who counts. Delegation means never getting caught up in lame, tedious, time-wasting "work." I create, and I delegate. That's all I do.

And while the delegating side of my brain berated my weak staff, the creative side of my brain got to thinking how very client-impressing a large bearskin rug and a stylishly taxidermied bear's head might look in the client-impressing outer lounge, or perhaps even more so in the deal-clinching inner lounge, behind the wet bar. I hear that a creative over at Vermion has a bear's paw humidor on his desk. Probably bought it at Crate & Barrel, or bearparts.com. But the point is, I heard about it. It made an *impression*, on a whole chain of jaded industry people linking that Vermion creative to me, and if Vermion's making an impression, then we'd damn well better be making a bigger one.

To make a long story short, I sweet-talked the Ups and the Veeps into bankrolling a little bear-bagging expedition for Image Team, under the excuse of "departmental bonding." They love teamwork, those Ups and Veeps. Teamwork is their mantra. In fact the senior partners fly to Thailand together each January for three weeks, to do coke and fuck hookers, as a team, and to strategize the future of the firm. That's how they bond. It's said that when a group of really rich men fuck the same hooker, it breaks down the masculine neuroses that prevent communication between them, and allows them to think and act as one, or some such faggitude. All I know is, this time next year I'm going to be on *that* team-building expedition and not this one. Because the Ups love me, and the Veeps are starting to hear good things about me, and when I plant a big black bearskin in the inner lounge — or maybe in the executive john, if it wouldn't get peed on — and when they see me sporting my new bionic foot, and I tell them the story of how I bagged that big one for the firm, well, that's going to make an impression that's just *huge*.

Still stuck. I tried wriggling, yanking, squirming. I can't feel my legs too clearly, but that's just fine considering. I'm biding my time, waiting for my opening. Mister Bear is fast asleep. I'd be asleep too, if Mister Bear didn't snore so incredibly loud. I thought animals were supposed to be silent, so they can't get snuck up upon and eaten by other animals. But bears don't worry about that, do they? Other animals don't fuck with bears. Bears rule the animal kingdom. Okay, I respect that. But I'm not from the animal kingdom, I'm from the United Fucking States. The animal kingdom is our colony. Mister Bear, you may think you're the carnivore and I'm the carne, but time will prove you wrong. Time will prove you a bear-burger breakfast and a soft warm place on the floor upon which to get nasty with Marcia from Product Dialogue.

Wish I could sleep. These pills are just a tiny bit speedy. That's usually how I like them. I think I've got some codeine in here someplace but I can't see at all, feeling slightly lightheaded under a Range Rover in the middle of the night in Noplace, Alaska. There's just the tiniest eau de petrol in the mix of hideous nature smells I'm choking on. But I'm cheerful, I'm upbeat.

It's funny … I used to fall asleep with a bear, a cuddly toy bear my parents gave me when I was small. He was a brown bear, and he wore reflective sunglasses and leather motorcycle clothes — the jacket, the hat and the chaps. He looked just like the singer in Judas Priest,

Rob Halford. I called him Bomber — Bomber Bear. Technically Bomber was my little brother Jimmy's bear, but Jimmy was too young to really appreciate bears. During the pre-divorce meltdown I used to have a lot of trouble getting to sleep and I really grew to depend on Bomber. So when I went off to live with Dad I appropriated him: I told Jimmy that Bomber had been killed in a motorcycle accident, and we had to bury him in a closed casket because his corpse was too mangled to look at, and we had held a nice funeral but we forgot to invite Jimmy, and Bomber never liked Jimmy anyway. Jimmy cried about that. Jimmy was a big crybaby, but we all cried a lot back then. So I said goodbye to Mom and Jimmy, and me and Bomber went to live with Dad in Orange County, and I slept with Bomber every night until the ninth grade when I found out Rob Halford is gay.

Knowing what I now know about bears, I think it's just sick that people give cute fuzzy stuffed gay ones to children. What are we teaching these kids? Bears aren't cute, they're not friendly or helpful, they're vicious, stupid, bloody-minded people eaters. You might as well teach children to play with infected rats, or foamy-mouthed doggies. I read tons of stories on the Internet during my extensive bear research phase about little kids climbing into bear cages at zoos to pet the bear, and getting mauled and eaten. Polar bears especially. I ask you, should we even be surprised? We're just setting kids up for that … *Look, mommy! See the bear? Oh, so cute, so white, so fluffy. Watch him dance. Back and forth, back and forth in his little home in the zoo. The bear looks sad. Why is he sad, Mommy? Does he not like the zoo? Maybe he is lonely, and needs love. I will hug him, Mommy, like I hug my own bear at home. Rrrrrrr … splat!* On my father's grave, on my mother's grave, on the graves of my bear-eaten subordinates and on the grave of my own foot I solemnly swear that when I get home I'm going to pitch the Ups and Veeps a public service campaign for children: Just Say NO to Bears! Reversing trends is my specialty and that one needs immediate, well-funded reversal. (We have to meet a public-service percentage every year anyway, ever since that whole Chinese lead paint dog chew mix-up and the accompanying class-action hell.) We'll need some kind of evil bear that kids can learn to fear, and some kind of hero figure — a hunter, or a ranger … no, even better: a talking car. A talking Sport-Utility Vehichle who will remind kids that nature is dangerous and bad! If it wasn't for society's deranged bear fetish and the conditioning I received from my parents, I probably wouldn't even be stuck here in this stupid mess. Thanks a lot, Mom.

I'm not getting depressed. Power of positive thinking. Power of yes! I am smart and lucky and sexy and cool and wealthy. I am edgy! I have good teeth and excellent taste! Good things happen to me. Because I make them happen. And because the universe loves me.

Tom Petty never seemed so deep and meaningful to me before. But somehow Tom Petty knew: the waiting really is the hardest part — especially when you're covered with crawling ants. But I can beat this. I'm a can-doer. I just have to bide my time. Someone will come, soon. Meanwhile I've got something here in my hand that feels about like I remember codeine feeling, plus another OxySufnix, in the unmistakable blister pack. A cold Bud, a Slim Jim and these pills, and then I'm going to try to get some shut-eye.

Getting rescued tomorrow. Big day ahead.

3

Asshole ate my other foot! This really impacts my outlook.

Oh, I was close. I was there! I was dancing in the end-zone. I would be angry, oh how pissed off I would be if my mood weren't so well-stabilized. I would be howling mad and probably depressed and blubbery too, maybe even weeping like a little girl, or trembling like a blind kitten in a sack falling towards the water ... man, you gotta love mood stabilizing drugs.

But can I at least describe this to you? How close I was? I woke up in the morning and Mister Bear was gone. Sensing an opening, I unsheathed my plan and plunged into action. From the snack box I extracted one Texas Pete's Yard-Long Spicy Chorizo Jerky Twister — the largest, longest, thickest and most satisfying beef jerky Texas has to offer — and bent one end of the stiff, sulfated meat into a crude hook. Using this wobbly meat-hook I reached out like a stoned croupier to rake in the jackpot: the jack! I hooked the knob of the jack crank, but it slipped free. I hooked it again, it slipped free, again and again ... but I did not give up, I persevered, because Marv Pushkin Gives Nothing to Nobody, and Especially Not UP! and finally, after eons of this, I somehow snagged the jerky in its scissor knee and oh so slowly, oh so carefully and gently began to reel it in across the lumpy, scrubby, muddy and buggy bog I've been lying in, soaking in, sinking into … thence to jack the fucking axle off my knees, thence to clamber into the cockpit, lock the door, load the gun, cue up the Slayer, crank up the seat-heater and the Shiatsutronic roto-massage system … oh, I could smell it!

And then Mister Giant Fat Stupid Snarling Vicious Ugly Malodorous Evil Angry Buzz-Killing Bear arrived out of nowhere, howling and screaming as if I was his girlfriend and the jack was his best friend from college. He charged, rammed the car hard — further crushing my knees, and somehow lowering this oil pan a centimeter closer to my face — and then he tried to squeeze under here with the rest of me, swiping with his paw, snapping his teeth … he almost got me.

He got the jack instead, and he also got the Jerky Twister. *My* Texas Pete's Yard-Long Spicy Chorizo Jerky Twister. Like my feet aren't good enough, that he has to raid my snacks as well. He's eating me *and* he's starving me.

But it's a funny thing: in the pantheon of jerky, there's chorizo, spicy chorizo, extra-spicy chorizo … and then, at the bottom of a smoking crater in the center of the room, there's Texas Pete's. Hotter Than The Sun™. Don't Mess With Texas™. Face-Melting Good™. (And it's no lie — it did actually melt a small child's face once, which is where Image Team got involved, and how I became a fan.)

Mister Bear gnawed on this yard-long cord of jerky napalm, appearing to enjoy it for maybe ten seconds … then he spat out half of it in a smoking gob of drool and began rubbing his face on his belly, huffing and puffing with his lips pulled back and his giant tongue flipping around, spraying bear-spit in all directions. He panted and spat and drooled and waddled around in a circle trying to cool down his lips. What a pussy! Take that, Mister Bear. Don't mess with Texas! I laughed out loud it was so funny.

Shortly after I started laughing at him he started eating my other foot. Who knew bears were so sensitive? Jesus, it almost hurt. I mean the pain is pretty much blocked but just the concept of the blocked pain existing down there somewhere in my leg, the crunching and the ripping and the being yanked on, it disturbs me slightly. But a great feature of OxySufnix is you can chew one up and get the whole twelve-hour timed release dosage in one hour of bliss. And that's where I am right now, floating on cloud nine while Sensitive Mister Bear lies on his belly a few feet left of the Rover, still rubbing hot chorizo oil off his lips. Sucker.

Mister Sensitive Bear, how smart are you really? I've read that you're "cunning" and "subtle"; I sure don't grasp your subtlety yet. Whenever someone cites me evidence of the intelligence of animals, they further convince me of the stupidity of humans.

Take dogs, for instance. Dogs are prized, by dog-prizers, for their intelligence. Edna's hyperactive Papillon, Wagner, never despairs of impressing me with his intelligence. He keeps bringing me his leash. When I enter the house, when I sit, when I stand, when I emerge from the bathroom, he picks up the little leather strap, symbol of his own slavery, and drops it drooly on my feet. He thinks maybe I'll take him for a walk so he can shit all over our nice neighborhood. Maybe he even thinks I'll buy him ice cream and a movie. I throw Wagner's leash in the closet, he brings it back. I throw the leash in the trash, he digs it out and brings it back. I kick him in the ribs, he brings the leash. I take the leash and whip him with it, he leaves me alone for maybe five minutes, then he brings the leash again.

Wagner exhibits no learning ability. A robot vacuum cleaner can grasp concepts this dog cannot grasp. He's deluded: he thinks he can make me his friend, make me throw his dog-spit-covered chew toys and scratch his hairy testicles and do all the other stuff that Edna does for him. I yell at Wagner, I step on Wagner, I pick him up and throw him, but he just won't comprehend my loathing. It's a very retarded kind of intelligence, if you ask me.

Mister Intelligent Bear, what's your S.A.T. score? Or did you take the Bear Aptitude Test? How did you do on Lumbering? What's your Snarling percentile? Do you have plans to further your bear education? I'd get further from here if I were you, Mister Bear. When those Search and Rescue guys show up with their big bear-killing guns, you're going to have a lot of flying lead to outwit.

Truth is, I don't even know how much of me you've eaten, because I can't see past this axle. But I'm a realist — or at least an opti-realist. I have to assume at the rate you've been gnawing on me I've lost quite a lot: tendons, little bones ... things they can't just graft from my earlobe. It's horrifying to contemplate, but it's a brutal fact that when I get out of here I'm going to have to buy some new feet. They'll be expensive, I'm sure, and time-consuming, but I've got time and Range Rover has lots of money, and my legal position is iron-clad, vis a vis the utter failure of this jack to provide reliable jacking in exactly the adverse jacking conditions Range Rover has repeatedly claimed their product easily overcomes, leading to undeniably severe injury and lifelong mental trauma. What jury wouldn't sympathize with a guy who lost his feet to a bear due to blatant manufacturer negligence? To the tune of several dozen million American simoleons, at least! I mean, who can put a price on feet?

So I've been thinking more about that human foot transplant. I'm sure they can do those now, in our futuristic era of high-tech medicine. I could end up with the feet of a professional athlete who died in a car crash after smoking too much marijuana. I wonder how high I could jump if I had basketball player feet? I'll probably get a new shoe size and have to buy a whole new set of shoes. That'll be fun. I live for shoes.

Only, they better not give me negro feet.

You know … prosthetic feet are kind of cool, too. In their way. For instance: there's a café in Belltown where I get my double latté in the mornings — only because there's a girl who works the espresso machine there who's kind of a dyke, but really really hot, so I go there to leer at her — and at this café I've often noticed this guy with prosthetic feet. Some kind of veteran, I guess. He's got nothing but aluminum and plastic from just below the knees all the way to the floor. He's kind of an older hippie looking guy. He usually wears tie-dyes and jogging shorts, a waxed grey mustache and his grey hair in a pony tail; he looks like shit, basically. But he can walk quite well, which is amazing if you think about it. He's a little bit overweight but not fat or anything, not Edna fat. At least he's trying. He's got little sport shoes on his little plastic feet and he takes his little pug dog out for a walk every morning. He stands, he sits, I even saw him jump up and down once when I knocked coffee in his lap. (I watched him fall over once, too. Actually I sort of pushed him, accidentally — or like, fifty percent accident, forty-nine percent enforcement of my personal space against hippies in general, and maybe just one tiny percent of curiosity about whether he could break his fall with those legs of his. Which he couldn't, and that was entertaining to watch, but mostly it was an accident.)

A guy like that, it's not fair to call him a cripple — or rather you could call him a cripple — in fact I must have called him a cripple at some point — but he's more than that, he's evolved beyond it. He's trans-crippled … he's Crippled Plus! Crippled Pro! A guy like that is an inspiration to a guy like me. I wonder how he lost his legs. I never thought to ask him … actually I never thought to speak to him at all, because he's a dirty hippie with metal legs. But me, I'd be different: I'd be clean and well-shaven, and I'd wear long Armani slacks, and I bet people wouldn't even be able to tell the difference. Because I've got *way* more legs left than that guy. In terms of legs remaining, that guy's not even in my league.

I wonder if a bear ate his legs, too. I can't wait to ask him!

It'll go like this: After an absence of several months, all the café regulars and the hot lesbian barista chick will have been wondering for some time: what ever happened to that stylish, sexy, edgy ad executive who used to grace them all with his presence every weekday morning for ten minutes or so? And then I'll just saunter right in with an air of mystery, nonchalance and trial-by-fire machismo, with a spring in my step and a smile on my face, saying nothing, betraying nothing, as if I'd never been gone. When the hot lesbian (bisexual?) barista chick asks where I've been keeping myself I'll tell her: Oh, you know, up in Alaska, hunting bears.

And she'll be strangely turned-on by the rugged, world-weary edge in my voice, the voice of a man who's stared down death. She may feel momentarily confused about her sexuality, but she won't notice my feet and the other regulars won't notice my shiny new feet, not at all. But *then*, as I gaze penetratingly into the now-blushing face of the hot barista chick who's sexually flexible, at the moment I drop a nickel suggestively in her tip jar ... our old friend Super Cripple will clank through the front door on his metal legs, his relatively antiquated and somewhat dumpy-looking aluminum legs, to get his morning coffee. He'll see me, and instantly, he'll know. He will spot with my first step that something has changed about me, and he'll look down at my shoes and see they're brand new, polished and of a different size than they used to be. Our eyes will meet, he'll raise an eyebrow, look me up and down and exclaim, "Dude ... nice feet!"

And that might be the beginning of an unlikely but long and lasting friendship, the kind of friendship one might eventually parlay into film rights. But then again probably not. Because I'm a busy guy and he smells like wheat grass juice, and if I tell him how I killed the bear that ate my feet he might get all liberal and indignant on me, and when hippies weep it's just embarrassing.

But still, he can give me some pointers in the early stages, as I learn to operate my new bionic feet, to walk and run and leap in them, to kick Wagner with them, to cross them up on my desk as I stretch out in my Aeron chair after a long day of creativity and delegation. I bet I could be a bad-ass kung fu master with my lightweight rock-hard titanium super feet.

I just have to somehow make sure they don't graft negro feet onto me. I wish I had a Sharpie, I could write WHITE FEET ONLY PLEASE on my arm or some place on my body where neurosurgeons would see it. My forehead, even. Just in case. Just in case I'm not conscious when they rescue me.

Which they definitely will do. Soon!

Look, don't get me wrong: negroes have excellent feet. Amazing feet. Look at Jesse Owens! Michael Jordan! (Actually it could be kind of cool to have Michael Jordan's feet, if I could have them certified and really prove to people, "Hey, these aren't just any negro feet, these are Michael Jordan's!" Imagine the cachet of that.) And even if they just gave me the feet of some semi-famous pro or college basketball playing negro I'm sure they'd be excellent feet in the practical sense, not inferior in any way, not funny smelling. My concern is purely an aesthetic one. I just want to *match*. I'm a man who takes care of himself, who works hard to look good at all times. Having negro feet would be like walking on to the tennis court of life in black socks, every day. It's beyond faux pas — it's well into freakshow. I wouldn't even know what box to check on the census any more. I'd be an other, a mixed. I'd be a decline to state.

Who was that detective with the claws instead of hands? Mister Claw? No ... J. J. someone. J. J. Arms. Yeah, there's a super-cripple for you. How did he lose his hands? Bears, probably. I wonder if he's still alive, fighting crime, solving mysteries, stabbing bad guys in the face with his claws. I could be just like that only I'd use kung-fu high-kicks on bad guys and save my hands for getting freaky with Marcia from Product Dialogue, in a tender erotic embrace on the bear skin rug in the executive bathroom.

I hope Marcia isn't along when they come to rescue me. I'd hate her to see me like this. Mauled, mud caked ... and yeah, one of the many awful smells you smell is me. I have soiled my wool hunting slacks and my Calvin Kleins. It had to happen, didn't it? I'm at peace with it, but I don't want Marcia to see me this way. I am not looking my sexiest right now. *So* not sexy. The image of me, steeped in blood and shit and Slim Jim wrappers, trapped and ... humiliated, really, by that dumb bear ... If Marcia sees me like this she'll never call me Daddy again.

HELP! A Bear is Eating Me!

4

I wonder if my darling Edna and Marcia from Product Dialogue have warmed to one another in my absence. They sure were frigid on each other in my presence. They didn't say a word to or about each other from Seattle to yesterday. I had them both in the Rover from Anchorage to Camp Image Team, with Edna attempting to navigate in the shotgun seat and Marcia sitting in the middle of the back seat, where the rear view mirror gave me an excellent view of her independent front suspension absorbing the off-road shocks. Marcia was quiet — one of her many luxury features. Edna was not quiet. She moaned and complained and worried and told me I was doing it wrong, whatever *it* happened to be.

"Marv, we are *not* on the map," she whined as I piloted my unstoppable Rover over fallen logs and mid-sized canyons. "You're going to get us stuck in some tree! What was wrong with that trail? It was a fine trail." I explained to her that a Range Rover creates its own trail automatically, by crushing objects directly beneath it. The in-dash navigation and luxury-management screen displayed an attractive nipple of concentric red rings undulating dead ahead of us, across a field of calm grey-green pixels and occasional suggestions to relax. Who needs trails when you've got Global Positioning? We were closing in on the agreed-upon spot, and it was important that I reach it first, both to humiliate Frink, who claims to know this area, and to win a certain bet over who sets up camp versus who sips cold beer on the self-inflating couch.

So we crushed our winning way through the undergrowth and overgrowth, efficiently trampling the scrawny brush and wetlands that passed for nature, making a bee-line for the prize. But Edna would not shut up about the "danger." I told her: baby, I had this car danger-sealed. Danger cannot enter, so baby, shut up.

Marcia from Product Dialogue whined: "Aren't you worried you might run over a squirrel?" Marcia has a weakness for small furry things. Which is great when those small furry things are sweaters or lingerie, but sometimes her weakness is just weak.

"Marcia," I explained, "just by driving a fossil-fuel burning car from the ferry station in Anchorage to here, we must have already killed twenty or thirty squirrels with global warming. Not counting all the bugs on the windshield, or that cat that Frink ran over at the Chevron. I mean, did you go vegan or something?"

"No," she said, submissively, the way I like. She pouted a little.

"Are you going off Atkins and switching to a cruelty-free diet?"

"No."

"Good. Cruelty looks good on you."

"Marv!" Edna complained. "What are you … that's a *cliff*, Marv! You're driving straight down a *cliff!*"

"Edna, do you even know what four-wheel drive means? Do you grasp the concept?"

"It won't mean *poop* if the car's upside-down, Marv!"

"We have a very low center of gravity, Edna. We're Velcroed to the land."

Looking in the mirror I noticed that quiet, stoic, beautiful Marcia from Product Dialogue appeared a little pale. She has such a delicate constitution, like a bird really, and it occurred to me that while Edna would be the one to complain and critique, Marcia would be more the type to spill her Alaskan motel breakfast all over my Oxford leather upholstery. So I stopped the car.

"Why are we stopped? What are you doing?" annoyed Edna.

"Rest stop. Map check. Piss break."

"On the face of a *cliff*? If I open this door I'll break my ankle and *die*!"

"It's not a cliff, baby. It's a ravine." I clambered out the drivers' side, onto about a 45 degree gravelly incline covered with saplings and scrub and big natural-looking rocks. When I slammed the door, the whole car slid downhill about a foot and the women inside screamed and clutched their seat belts. Priceless. I gave them a wink and a thumb up and hiked up the hill and back a bit, just far enough so a sudden wind wouldn't blow my urine on the Rover.

God, what a beautiful car I own. It's really in its element out here, gleaming chrome and gunmetal grey against the blue sky, a lovely patina of authentic off-road mud on its flaps, undergrowth caked beneath the real chrome bumper like the rouge on a lawnmower's lips, and a long flat trail of subjugated vegetation and churned turf blazing off into the distance behind. I've never seen my car looking happier than it did that day, like a free-roaming alpine goat perched on a rocky bluff, sniffing the wind for other goats' vaginas. I wish I could find another really hot car for my car to mate with, I love it so. It's got a look that screams *Money!* but it screams in a classy, operatic voice that's also rugged and Teutonic, sort of a Conan the Singing Barbarian scream, if you follow me. Basically, it makes everybody inside of it seem wealthy and sophisticated, yet violent. Through the polarized rear window, even Marcia and Edna looked poised and regal, sitting still, clutching their seat belts, leaning uphill, doing and saying nothing. Except I knew Edna was seething. She likes to seethe. And when Edna seethes, Marcia pouts. It's cute, really.

I finished peeing all over nature and returned to the Rover. We slid a few more inches downhill when I slammed the door.

"Marv, are you *trying* to get us killed?" Edna bitched.

"Not entirely," I said.

"Remember? Remember what the doctor said about *impulses*? Don't you think you're acting just a *teensy* bit self-inflictive?"

I threw it in low gear and put the hammer down. The wheels spun as we slid farther down the ridge, flinging rocks and twigs in all directions. Marcia from Product Dialogue let out the tiniest little whimper, like she does when she comes. Sexy!

"That's crazy talk, baby. I love me. I would never hurt me." I rocked the steering wheel left, then right, sort of randomly plowing around the gravel we were swimming in, trying to drill down into something bite-able. The car slid and twisted around in place like a hovercraft, throwing up an epic cloud of dust around us as the engine roared with automotive excellence. Finally we snagged something and sprang, caribou-like, up the side of the so-called cliff and back on to boring flat land — where I just barely

spotted some little surprised animal dart under the front
wheels, a beaver or dog or something, I don't know what
exactly but the girls had their eyes closed so I decided to
neglect to mention it — and there we were, horizontal
again, "safe."

Marcia squealed with delight and clapped her little
hands together. Edna rolled her eyes.

Edna: "Maybe *you* should go vegan, Marv. Just
drive to the supermarket and back, hunting tofu."

"Baby? Did you smoke crack while I was out there
with Walter?" Edna huffed. Marcia giggled. (I should
explain: Walter, obviously, is my cock; Edna knows this;
Marcia also knows this; Edna does not know Marcia
knows this. Or maybe it was dawning on her, but that was
starting to matter less and less as we got deeper into Bear
Country.)

"Vegans have ethics, Marv. They care about
others."

"I care about others. I care how they taste!"
Badda-bing! I crack myself up. But no giggle from
Marcia ... no, I suppose Marcia actually cares about
others from time to time herself. Silly girl. In the mirror I
saw her little mini-pout, eyebrows slightly furrowed, head
bent forward, chin pointing down toward her slender neck
and her big, tight funbags jutting from the underwire bra
and the camo lycra action halter I bought her. Her body
said Fuck Me Sideways, but her face said Apologize First.

"Hey, ladies, listen, I have a lot of respect for
nature," I lied. "Why do you think I brought you out
here? Look out the window! This is nature! The
grandeur and the mystery and the cuteness all here in
front of us now. We came here to pay our respects to
Mother Nature, and to rediscover our human relationship

with her."

"Oh, I'm relieved," sneered Edna. "All this time I thought you came up here to shoot guns at bears."

"Baby, that *is* the human relationship. Hunting is a nature thing. Animals hunt other animals, or else they hunt plants, but everything hunts something. As hunters we must respect our prey, get to know them, study them, learn from them. Hunting brings us closer to nature, that's just a fact."

"Marv, you're not honestly going to *eat* this bear?"

"Baby we are going to skin, clean, fillet, marinate and barbecue this bear, yes. No part will be wasted. We will take no more than we need in order to have an authentic bear-hunting experience, and then we will respectfully leave this place and return to the city to share the wisdom we have gained," I said. Or some such bullshit.

"What does bear taste like?" enthused Marcia from Product Dialogue.

"The pizzle," I said, "is considered a delicacy."

There was no more grousing after that. Soon enough the dashboard chimed succinctly to announce we had reached the coordinates of the official Alaskan Bear Baiting Station — just a clearing with a metal sign nailed to a tree, proclaiming it as such — and yes, we got there first! I stepped from the gleaming Rover, tossed a few business cards on the ground, and claimed the camp in the name of the Image Reversal Team of Wilson & Saunders Market Strategies. Marcia and Edna headed off to opposite sides of the clearing while I popped open a cold Budweiser, unloaded the self-inflating couch and waited patiently for it to self-inflate.

Marcia and Edna. What a riot. If I were in a hospital recovering from exotic neurosurgery, and you were a biographer for a large publishing house, sent to capture the exciting story of my trial by bear, perhaps you'd ask why I chose to handicap a perfectly legitimate hunting trip by including a couple of jelly-kneed women who don't even enjoy killing. You might wonder, as some members of Image Team no doubt wonder, why, of all useless jelly-kneed PMS-ing bitches, I would choose to bring that burbling font of aggravation which scientists call Edna. But especially you have to be wondering, why would I bring both my so-called "life partner" *and* my under-the-radar fuck? In the same car, no less?

Well … I can't exactly tell you. Not yet. But I can tell you this:

Marcia from Product Marketing came along because I told her to come, and she does what I tell her to do, which is the cornerstone of our relationship and what makes her such an excellent fuck. She is a whore of the finest caliber. She sucks it, she takes it in the ass, I can slap her, I can dress her up and boss her around, I can stick it in every hole and she takes it squealing. She is tight and round and versatile, and compliant. Frankly, I am addicted to fucking Marcia from Product Dialogue. She's a sex-pill I must take regularly to relieve the crushing stress of delegation. And I mean regularly — I put her on birth control just so she'd quit bleeding on me every month, so I could still fuck her on schedule without ruining my Calvin Kleins. There's no way I could survive a week away from civilization without a Marcia to fuck. Especially with Edna on board.

Edna I do not fuck. I used to, for years. I know Edna's vagina like I know my own driveway. But I've moved on from there. Edna's vagina is neither tight nor versatile, and especially not compliant. Edna's vagina is as kinky as a cold bowl of oats. There was a time, back in the halcyon days of early wedlock, when for some reason cold-oat-bowl sex seemed intimate and charming. Back then I had just caught hold of the first rung of the ladder to the top, I was young and starry-eyed with a huge future to offer, and Edna was young and pretty and had a large inheritance. From the moment I met her, I knew she'd buy me things, if I could just embrace that cold bowl of oats deep inside her. I suppose I knew someday I'd be able to afford my own things, but I just couldn't wait. I'm impatient, and I love things. And I suppose at times it wasn't hard to pretend that she was good enough. She used to be sweet, and quiet, and less fat.

But oh, how the world turns. While Edna has grown tiresome, I've grown strong. I'm high up on that ladder of success with a clear shot at the top rung, and I'm most handsomely compensated. Oh, the things I can buy! Such fine things, and so many of them. My Rover. My fine clothing. My luxury condominium in Bainbridge. My guns. My porno. Tight furry slut-pants for Marcia. Budweiser by the truckload, Slim Jims by the mile.

Is it really my fault? I wouldn't be so obsessed with money if there wasn't so much great stuff for sale. I blame society. And this story of mine, this ordeal under this car versus that bear, is going to net me seven figures, easy. I bet the Disney Channel snaps it up for one of their nature specials. Should I settle for seven figures? I wouldn't start there, but could I settle there? I think not. There's going to be all the collateral as well, the books and cartoons, plush toys, Happy Meals, that stuff's worth a lot. But if we could piggyback the Say No To Bears campaign onto a Disney nature special, I might be willing to settle for seven figures. Because nobody reaches kids like Disney. Disney owns kids. Disney and I could do crazy things to kids.

But that's assuming that the Rover lawsuit settles early out-of-court, so my neurosurgeons are getting paid. That's the important thing: I want the best treatment. I want the Tiger Woods of Neurosurgery working on my feet. I want —

Shh!

Someone's coming!

HELP! A Bear is Eating Me!

5

I heard it. If you were real you would have heard it too. Someone stepping through old twigs and undergrowth, someone coming through the trees, they are coming to save me they are coming RIGHT NOW! All right! About fucking time, too! I'm trying to yell HELP but my voice is a little stuck. But I hear it.

It's not just me. Mister Bear hears it too. He's up on all fours now, waving his nose in the air and growling low from deep in his hairy guts. I'm yelling OVER HERE and no sound is coming out of my mouth. I'm screaming BEAR! Can they hear me? I'm so close! Why can't I speak? I can cough at least. Cough cough cough! COUGH!

Mister Bear is scampering away. Is that his fear-scamper or his hunger-scamper? I've got to make some kind of signal. I'll rap this empty beer can against the tailpipe. Rap rap rap rap rap! Cough cough cough! Three coughs means I'M OVER HERE. Five raps means BEAR WARNING!

Did I hear it again? Yeah! There, I heard it. Definitely coming closer, this is working, I'm a genius, rap cough rap cough rap rap rap! If I could just figure out how to scream … over here, yes! Follow your nose to the smell

45

of human blood, gasoline, shit and fine Oxford leather upholstery. You are getting warmer. I hear you, you are getting very toasty. *Hot, you're hot! You're on fire, baby! I see you!* Over on my right, at the edge of the clearing, peering in! You are down on your hands and knees, carefully checking for predators. You must be a Forest Ranger. You are wearing a large fur parka … and a furry hat …

No you're not. You're a bear. Another fucking bear. A second, separate, extra, additional fucking bear.

Great! You know I almost ran out of fucking bears for a second there! I was down to just the one fucking bear, and when he ran off I didn't know how I was going to meet my fucking bear requirements, my being attacked and eaten requirements, my savage predator from hell requirements. But three cheers for Alaska, they've got 24-hour hot fucking bear delivery.

Note to self: Nuke Alaska.

Now this new bear is standing up, I can't even see his head from under here. He's big. A grizzly, this one. Big and brown. Quiet, though, not an asthma sufferer like Mister Bear. He's looking around, he's sniffing, he sniffs the car, does he sniff me?

He sniffs me.

I'm going to take an OxySufnix now.

He's coming on over. Shit, he's just enormous. Smelly, too. He's sniffing the ground but his head alone is so large that I can't see the top of it. I wonder if I have another Spicy Chorizo Jerky Twister in this box.

Now he's going around behind me. Where is he? What's he doing?

No! He's peeing on the Rover! Goddammit, I think I might actually be losing my placid inner balance here. Squirt squirt squirt, I hear the stream hitting the mudguard and dripping on the ground, and surprise! It reeks, utterly, of bear.

Fucking bear the second: you may rule nature but this Rover is *mine*. It is my castle and my kingdom, and you shall rue the day you urinated upon that which is Mine. Come on over here and try the Spicy Chorizo, you stupid fat northern handbag.

I wish I had some poison in my pillbox, something really deadly like botox or botulism or sarin that I could dose a Slim Jim with and feed it to the bears. I read that raw meat can develop botulism just by being left out for one day. I've been left out two days; maybe my legs will develop botulism and Mister Bear will be poisoned by them.

The big brown furry fuckwad's over on my left now. His paws are so much larger than my head. Toes the size of my hands. He's got some reach.

C'mere you … what bear can resist Texas Pete's Spicy Chorizo Jerky Twister? Here, I'll unwrap it. There, I'll toss it where you can see it.

He's interested … he's nosing it. Mmm, aromatic isn't it? Smell the chorizo. Taste the sulfites. Feel the burn. He's licking it … yes, eat the jerky! Yes! He's eating it! Sucker! He's chewing the whole thing, he's gnawing it up good. Hah! He's swallowing it. He's licking his big bear lips and his huge bear teeth.

He looks like maybe he wants another one.

Great. Welcome to Marv's Alaskan Bear Bistro and Snack Bar. I'll be your maitre'd and entree this afternoon. I'm sorry sir, there are no tables available under the Rover, but please allow us to seat you in the Leg Room. Please do not enter the kitchen while the chefs are hiding. No, honestly sir … no, these snacks are reserved! Why do you want Slim Jims when there's perfectly good Leg of Marv over there? No! Get away! Cough cough! Rap rap!

Hey, what was that noise? An animal, a scream. A bear scream from way over there. Jesus, I'm parked on the bear freeway.

But no, I'd know that asthmatic voice anywhere … it's good old Mister Bear himself, back from the 7-Eleven with Slurpees and a video. And just like that, Big Brown is backing off from my snack box and stepping away from the vehicle.

Mister Bear, could it possibly be that I'm glad to see you?

Now they're back behind my head where I can't see. But I can hear the growling and smell the bear whiz. I smell a bear fight.

There they are, on the left. Big Brown — oh shit, now that I see them side by side he's twice as big, easily — he's advancing on Mister Bear who's backing slowly away … now he's stopped, he's on his hind legs, snarling like a jet plane taking off underwater, scrunching his bear face into a wrinkled, toothy scowl. And now … he leaps! Straight through the air and right at Big Brown and they're wrestling like cats!

Bear fight! Bear fight! Bear fight! Oh, this is incredible. I have to get a shot of this with my phone, where's my phone, here it is. Shit, they've stopped. C'mon bears, fight some more. Over to the left a little.

Oh jeez, the blood. Mister Bear took a hit there, right down the shoulder. But Big Brown got clawed in the face, oooooh … the eye. The former eye.

Big Brown's backing off … he's turning … he's walking away. Mister Bear charges at him, screeching and snapping, and Big Brown scurries into the forest like a frightened Papillon. Ladies and Gentlemen … it's Mister Bear in the first round!

Incredible. I'm tingly with extreme-sports-feel. Wow. Did you see my bear kick that other bear's ass? That other bear that was twice my bear's size? My bear is awesome. Mister Bear, you're a madman! You're a monster! You saved my snacks! You're my hero! Mister Bear, do you want a beer? Let me buy you a beer. Man, you have got to be the meanest, baddest and most omnivorous bear in all of Alaska! You are king, Ichiban, number one! You wear the belt, you pose with the swimsuit models. Woo-hoo!

Hey, I said that! Hey, I'm saying this! I can say! Mister Bear you have not only vanquished our common foe, you have also cured my laryngitis. Is there no limit to your awesome power? Are you sure you don't want a Bud? Here, I'll open it for you. Interested? No? Okay, I'll have one. Do you want a Slim Jim? No? Here, this one isn't spicy, it's Country Turkey and Cheese. Not interested? Well, is there anything, anything at all I can get you?

Oh … you want that?

Yes, of course, I forgot … you're eating me.

Well all right, go ahead. I already wrote off everything south of the axle. Let's just — OUCH! Let's … let's make a deal: I'm all yours from the knees down, but please, after that, at least *try* the Slim Jims. After that you've got to stop because the rest of me is not sitting under a car, and I suspect the pressure of the axle on my legs is acting like a really expensive luxury tourniquet, I think that's why I haven't yet bled to death. But if you eat me on this end I'll bleed like crazy and not only will that be impossible to get out of my brand new suede hunting attire, but also I'll die. And I'll be dead and we won't have this special relationship of ours any more. You'll be all alone out here with no one to eat or talk to. And I'll start to go bad and develop botulism, and then you'll die from eating me after I've been left out too long.

We're not so different, you and I. We both dominate. We both kick ass. We both have excellent taste. You are eating me, for instance, and I would eat you, too. I will eat you. Don't forget, I'm still going to win. But you are a worthy opponent, Mister Bear. I salute you. In a different time and a different place I'm sure we would have been great friends.

6

Oh science, oh technology, oh medicine and pharmacology, how much do I love you? Let me count … OxySufnix, Percoset, Anctil, Smarmex: you take the pain away and bring me cool fluffy clouds and ultimate smoothness. Performil, Septihone, Winnerol: you remove my doubts and confusion and give me clarity. Sombutol, Codeine, Abnap: you tuck me in and turn out my lights. Ritalin, Rapidol, Viagra, Crystal Methedrine: you put my pedal to the metal. There's no feeling I ever wanted to feel that the alchemists of modern pharmacy don't already have a pill for. Drugs, I'm so glad you're here with me. I couldn't do this without you. It was very smart of me to stock up on you in Vancouver, where you are available so cheaply and without a prescription.

Of course I *have* a prescription. I'm not some twitchy pill-popper. I have several good doctors telling me to take this stuff. That's how I know they're good doctors. Edna dragged me one time to see this bad doctor, a real quack, who tried to prescribe me some analysis, some deep probing of my past, some couch time. I told this doctor, Hey Doctor, do you know who I am? I'm Marv Pushkin, and I'm stunningly important! Do I look like I have time to lie there in the greasy indentation left on your fake leather couch by the fat asses of a hundred depressive clients of yours, telling you private details from my fabulous life? You wish! If you don't have a pill for whatever you're diagnosing me with, then maybe you should diagnose me with something else, something more physical and real and less effervescent and psychological and gay. I'm not paying $100 an hour to sit around un-medicated in your office and weep — boo hoo hoo — about my funny urges and my goofy outbursts and my wacky, zany, nutty "problems." If I'm sick, I have an illness, not a "problem." Nobody has "problems" any more, they have pills for that now. So give me the pill or tell me who will.

So the pain pills, obviously, are for my pain. What pain? I haven't felt real painful pain in years. Pain, to me, is like an unsolicited e-mail from my nervous system, trying to sell me something I'm not even slightly interested in. I might read it if I'm bored, otherwise I trash it with a single click. Right now those e-mails are really stuffing my inbox, but I'm ignoring them.

I remember the bad old days of pain, pain that hurt. I had these headaches, sure, once upon a time. That was some real pain. Do you imagine being eaten by a bear is painful? Imagine instead if a tiny rodent, a rat with long teeth and sharp scratching claws, woke up in the center of your brain and started burrowing its way out your face. Imagine pain you can hear, crawling around inside your skull with every twitch of your eyebrow, searing the inside of your head like acid. Imagine your head is one big tooth, and it's got an abscess. Oh yes, it was bad, but now it's good, oh yes. I can hardly imagine pain now. I'm so *over* pain, thanks to OxySufnix. OxySufnix, I owe you a beer.

Then there was that other problem, the one that quack doctor wanted to apply couches to. I wasn't

depressed or anything, I was just great. I had been
taking the OxySufnix for six months and life was good,
I was high on life, life and OxySufnix. I mean, I'm even
better now, but really I was fine then. I felt excellent, so
excellent that one day, carried away in general enthusiasm,
I playfully emptied my 9mm Glock 19 all over the house
and did a lot of damage, shot holes in some fairly valuable
possessions, burned some stuff, I just went, I went, I
went, well not nuts. Never went nuts. I felt just fine, I
enjoyed the heck out of the whole process. I just wanted
to blow off some steam, see, and I did exactly that, but
in retrospect I admit I blew a little too hard. The glass
shower stall, the mirror, I got fairly scratched up. (Thank
you OxySufnix for blocking the pain.) I guess when
Edna got home I was not looking my best. Fell off my
usual tip-top condition, I guess, and I had bled all over
the new white Venetian shag carpet among all the other
damage, and Edna, dammit, got all hysterical and called
an ambulance, and that really pissed me off. I mean, how
humiliating is that? For Christ's sake Edna, just drive
me to the hospital and leave the paramedics out of our
living room, would you? But no, not Edna, she needs
everything *dramatic*. A frustrated actress, you see. So Edna
locked herself in the bathroom and dialed 911, and once
you dial 911 they just don't stop coming: cops, firemen,
paramedics, lawyers, gossip columnists, they swarm in like
flies and track blood all over the Venetian shag, and if you
happen to be *holding a pistol* for any reason — I was merely
trying to get the bathroom door open so I could calmly
explain to Edna what an utter cunt she was being and
what happens to people like that when they fuck around
with Marv Pushkin — then they, the nice home-invaders
who are ruining your rug, get extremely tense and rude

with you, and then if you try to relax them by *putting down* the pistol they all of a sudden tackle you and manhandle you and Taser the shit out of you, treating you like a fucking criminal in your own fucking luxury condominium!

Looking back on it now, I think that was the beginning of the end for me and little Miss 911-Dialing Driveway Snatch. She rode with me and two cops and two paramedics to the hospital, and because she knew she was in trouble, *serious* trouble, she toned down the hysteria a bit when they took her official statement, leaving out some of the unofficial, off-the-record statements I had made in the heat of the moment which might have been misconstrued. Me, I got a lot of stitches, a lot of bandages, and then for two days I got Observed.

But of course they had to let me out after 48 hours, because I'm not crazy. And if I was crazy I'd be the kind of devious super-crazy who can still convince shrinks that he's not crazy. And that's just what I did. I had the blond doctor with the Nazi spectacles, Dr. Plank, eating out of my hand. *Oh Doc, the pressure I've been under at the office!* (Hah.) *Oh, society's rigid expectations!* (Guffaw.) *I've realized I need to sit down and re-evaluate my life.* (Hardy har har.) And when Edna came to visit, I laid it on so thick I almost choked to death on my own acting. *Edna ... baby ... please don't leave me ... I need you so bad ... what a monster I've been ... please help me to get better ... I love you. I love you!* (Chortle!)

But meanwhile ... the awkward truth is I don't know why I did it any more than anybody else does. I did it for kicks, the fun factor, the pure fucking blast of shooting stuff up indoors, watching it explode when you point at it, being the sweet angel of annihilation, dealing judgment to appliances and furniture. Sure, I enjoyed the heck out of myself, but afterwards I kind of wished I hadn't shot my

brand-new flat screen LCD cinema display TV, because
I had been enjoying watching porno on it. And why did
I shoot up my ivory and teak minibar? All that perfectly
good scotch, and all those national league football mascot
shot glasses I collected in college, all destroyed. And above
all, why did I shoot up my Camero? I loved that car, and
when the guys at the shop said it was totaled, from nothing
but ten or twenty bullets out of a little nine millimeter
Glock and a few swings with a putting iron, when they told
me that buying a new Camero would be way cheaper than
fixing mine, that was when I realized I, Marv Pushkin, had
made a Mistake. And I didn't know why. So I went back
to the blond doctor with the Nazi glasses, and told him I
wanted some pills to help me never do anything like that
again.

And man, that doctor changed my life. I know it
sounds corny, but with Performil and Septihone, I simply
feel great all the time. It's that good. I always know what
to do, and I always do it. I have no more fear, no more
uncertainty. I am brave and wise and quick and clever.
Nothing bothers me. No storm can ripple the mirror-like
surface of the pond of my mood. If there's one thing in
life I can't live without, it's the two-pill combination of
Performil and Septihone. The Winnerol is really more
recreational, I get those from one of the custodians in our
building, really a very nice wetback, he's got a little side-
job dealing various pills. Sometimes I take a Winnerol
when I have to meet with particularly lame clients,
'cause it significantly decreases my boredom with their
shitty products, their retarded ideas and their agonizing
PowerPoint. And Ritalin is great for deadlines. But
Peformil, Septihone and OxySufnix, that's my trifecta of
feelgood.

I hope I took enough. Truth be told, I'm not totally certain what I'm taking right now because my vision has gone a little bit blurry. Which is normal, of course, with this much OxySufnix. And it's dark again, and I spilled my stupid pillbox. It just slipped out of my fingers while I was opening it, and now all these pills are lying in the mud beside me and honestly they all look about the same when you can't see anything. Except thankfully the OxySufnix comes in a square tinfoil blister pack, even J. J. Armes could find those, even if he was blind. So, block that pain … and I'll just take two or three of these other ones and hope for the best. If I feel bad, I'll take some more.

Meanwhile: the bear, he sleeps tonight. Ever since the big match he's been curled up next to the car. He spent a couple hours licking himself earlier, that was sure something to see. It's like the Nature Channel under here. I actually think he's warming me up a bit with his body heat. Small consolation for what he smells like.

A little-known bear fact: they reek! Somehow in all my research I never uncovered this salient info. They reek like giant sweaty socks full of pustulous ingrown toes, their piss smells like rotten vegetables and sulphur, they've got fish breath and their feet are caked with feces. I can't believe I was going to eat one. As it is, I think we're going to have to wrap up this bear in Dub-L-Tuf plastic garbage bags for the ride home if we don't want to get pulled over for stinking. I sure hope Javier and his cute little kids can get the bear stench off my car. When I get home, when I get rescued …

What is the holdup with that, anyway? Okay, thinking opti-pessimistically, suppose Baumer led Image Team out into the forest to look for me, and they were all eaten by bears. Suppose that happened yesterday. Still, Marcia and Edna would have stayed back at camp to pout and seethe. And being women, they would be cowering in a car, where I hope they'd have the brains to shut the windows and try not to smell like bear food. But at what point do they decide, when nobody comes back because bears have feasted upon their weak, indecisive entrails, at what point will they figure out the thing to do is to go get proper HELP? Search & Rescue, have you heard of them? Do you have any idea what they do? They search! And then they rescue! What idiot would undertake to search for and rescue me without the aid of Search & Rescue? Let's say the girls wait for a whole day and then they finally go get HELP. So tomorrow will be the day, tomorrow morning, the sky will be full of HELP in helicopters and seaplanes, searching for me and my car. HELP has infra-red SUV detectors! HELP has smart binoculars! HELP has upholstery-sniffing basset hounds! I'm not even hard to find, just follow the tire tracks from camp to my car. There's not even any searching involved, just follow the line in the mud.

Oh look, it's starting to rain.

HELP! A Bear is Eating Me!

7

BIGGER THAN BEARS: The Marv Pushkin Story!

Chapter Seven: **RESCUE AT LAST!**

The next morning as the first stinging rays of the
Alaskan sun found me bravely dying beneath my mighty
Rover, despairing of seeing ever again my sweet, loving
office or feeling the warm embrace of my condominium,
as I held back a mighty tsunami of tears with the last
strength in my desperate eyelids, clinging boldly to my
dwindling rations of hope ... all at once I heard a sound,
the sweetest sound I'd ever known: the sound of my own
name, shouted out in the forest. A search party! Using
a combination of loud coughs and elaborate beer can
rapping, I announced myself to the Alaskan Forest SWAT
Ranger Search & Rescue team. But as these brave men
approached my position, I warned them (via morse
code) that my ferocious captor would not easily offer
up his trophy. Indeed, just then, from out of nowhere,
the crazed predator I'd come to know as Mister Bear
charged furiously at the phalanx of rescue professionals,
his muscular thighs pumping with ursine fury, an
ancient battle-snarl echoing from his inhuman, animal,

mammalian, beary snout!

They mowed him down instantly in a blistering hail of high-powered ammunition. "Don't worry. Mr. Pushkin," the bald-headed mustachioed Ranger-in-chief told me as he stuck his head under the car to survey my wounds, "the bear's head is still intact, and I'm sure your Seattle taxidermists can patch up the pelt."

Then as the Forest SWAT Ranger Squadron Leader called back to base on his high-powered two-way radio, the other SWAT Rangers jacked up my Rover with military precision, being very respectful of the paint, and polished the mud and grime off the axle. Luckily, these Rangers were accompanied by a team of Search & Rescue field neurosurgeons who fit me with a remarkable pair of self-tightening "smart tourniquets", the newest thing from Japan. They stemmed the loss of blood while preventing gangrene and gently massaging my raw, exposed neurons.

"Oh Marv, you're so brave!" oozed Marcia from Product Dialogue, looking succulent in a tight halter-top and shorts. She wore a dainty clothespin over her nose. "I just can't stand the stench of those nasty evil bears! They swarmed over camp like bees! They ate Edna, they ate Harvey and Jim and the others, oh gosh it was awful! Hold me, Marv!"

So I held her, and she felt good, damn good, her warm, heaving bosom, her trembling chin. I kissed her, and squeezed her ample posterior. "If I hadn't been fixing my makeup in the truck," she trembled, "they would have got me too! So I asked myself, what would Marv do? And I decided to drive back to the ranger station, and I brought the best Search & Rescue team in all Alaska! I can't live without you, Marv, and neither can Image Team!"

As Marcia clutched my hand in hers, the SWAT

Rangers and their neurosurgical attaché lifted me onto a
sumptuously upholstered stretcher and carried me over
to have a look at Mister Bear. There, lifeless in the mud,
lay my tormentor, the killing spark snuffed from him. This
crumpled ball of meat and insulation had for nearly a
week toyed with my life, my being, my very existence as a
small Papillon dog might toy with a goat tendon. And yet,
I felt no hatred, no anger. I felt only the soothing rush of
relief and the bracing flush … of Victory.

"Violence begets violence, my ursine friend," I said.
Then I borrowed a Benelli M2 semiautomatic shotgun
from one of the Rangers and pumped a few more rounds
into his lifeless body, while they took pictures.

The doctors gave me an injection, a fundamentally
excellent injection, an injection of pure health and
restitution, pain relief and succor. Then the loud chopping
of a Red Cross SWAT Ranger Search & Rescue helicopter
began to macerate the air around us as its gleaming white
belly of aerospace aluminum floated overhead. A life-
saving hook was winched down to us, and the SWAT
Ranger medics carefully secured my stretcher to it.

"Thank you brave sirs," I screamed over the howl
of the chopper blades, "but what about those killer bears?
Something must be done! They're a menace to peaceful
humans like us."

"You're quite right, Mr. Pushkin," replied bald,
rippling, mustachioed, ex-Marine looking SWAT Ranger
Jock Thrustsworth — ten year veteran of the Alaskan
Bear Wars. "We've tried to live in balance with nature long
enough. This time, nature went *too far*. As soon as you
and your fiancé are safely out of here, I'm calling in an air
strike to napalm this whole forest."

I agreed it was the humane thing to do. He

signaled the chopper to raise the winch, but just then Marcia threw her warm, supple, heaving body on top of mine. "Oh Marv, I want to go with you! I hate this place!" she sobbed.

"Be brave, baby. I need you to skin and clean that bear before this whole forest goes up in well-deserved flames. Here, you'll need my Leatherman Super Tool."

"Oh Marv … I'm so hot for you!" she moaned, grinding against me passionately.

"But Marcia … could you ever love a man with no feet?"

"Darling, you're in luck! A white male college basketball player died of food poisoning in Anchorage just a few hours ago. They're saving the feet for you!"

"See you at the office, butterbuns!" I held her tongue in mine, and then she let go and the winch lifted me higher and higher up into the beautiful blue Alaskan sky, up into the clouds. And then I knew, finally, that my ordeal was over and everything was going to be fine. Sure, I had grown and changed, learned some important lessons about life, had an "arc" … but I was still Marv, Last of the Pushkins, and I had prevailed. Knowing that, I closed my eyes and allowed sleep to eat me.

The next morning I woke up lying in a cold puddle pinned under an SUV that stinks of bear piss. Shit. Nice dream, though. It could still happen.

I'm bored, is the problem now. Three days under a car and I've already run out of things to do. I polished all the mud off the exhaust and the suspension and all the other weird car parts down here, frankly I did a much, much, much more meticulous cleaning than Javier and his family ever did. When I get home I'll just point him to this spot and tell him to make the rest of it like that. And I tried some stretching exercises, but I might as well stretch a corpse. There's not enough room to get any kind of a real workout. I tried abdominal crunches and almost ripped my nose off on the oilpan plug. And then I passed out.

If I ever do return to the Alaskan wilderness, I'm bringing more games on my phone. I actually played Minesweeper for an hour this morning, that's how bored I am. Such a tedious game, and my fingers are so damn cold and numb I blew myself up every time. If there was one stupid cell tower anywhere in all of backwards Alaska I could not only dial 911 and be rescued, I could also download some new video games to play while I waited. Or ring tones. Or text messages. Or check my e-mail.

Or surf the web for some porn. I haven't been to MonsterBlackTorpedoes.com in weeks, I bet they have a new series up: video of negroes with cocks as big as my arm, stuffing it into the suffering cunts of tiny weeping blond women while swearing at them in gangsta rap lingo, calling them "ho-bags" which I'm sure they are. God, I miss the Internet. I never could find the kind of porn I really like until the Internet. I don't go for just any old porn, I'm very discriminating, but there's something really iconic and pure about MonsterBlackTorpedoes. com. Those women are skinny and pale, but the way they scream you'd think they're giving birth, and you know they're not faking it. It's got to hurt, but they take it, because they want it. Or else because they're junkies who need money for drugs, but still, they must want it a little bit, or else they'd get real jobs.

Man, I'm frozen stiff. Literally. Several pints low of blood, but I've somehow got a hard-on that won't quit. That dream about Marcia … oh, no wonder I'm horny, I haven't boned Marcia in three days! I'm going through sex withdrawal. As if I didn't have enough problems! When I get out of here I'm going to fuck Marcia in the ass so hard she'll be cross-eyed with carpet burns. That'll teach her to take three whole days to rescue me. Stupid whore. She'll love it, too.

Y'know, I would jack off right now just to warm up a little, just to kill a little fragment of this waiting … but what would Mister Bear say? Is he awake? Mister Bear? Hey bear! Are you around? No? Gone again? Probably off fucking some other bear. I read in my bear research that there's between 2 and 5 female black bears for every male, because the males are hunted more, because they're larger. So a bad-ass dominator like Mister Bear must get some sweet bear loving from the hot & heavy fem-bears out here. Oh yeah, humping a bear … that must be epic. The earth must shake. Give her some from me, my friend.

But I can't jack off, I don't have a towel or anything, do I? It's bad enough I crapped my pants, but if they find me with cum all over my jacket they might get some funny ideas about some gay tryst between me and Mister Bear. I can just see it: *forensic evidence suggests that Mr. Pushkin was erotically drawn to the bear's embrace.* Like one of those Internet furry cartoon suit pervs. None for me, thanks. I mean, I appreciate fine furs, especially on Marcia, but when I'm poking Marcia I'm not pretending to poke Rocky the Flying Squirrel.

Hello, Walter. How are you weathering the ordeal? Bloody but unbowed, I see. Shit, I must have taken a Viagra! That's the only explanation for your sudden improvement in posture. Ooh, you're warm and I'm cold.

But no, I am not getting Marv-jizz all over my camel hair hunting jacket. The blood and the mud and the other stuff that Edna spilled on me, it's just so un-Maxim, so non-Esquire. It's decimating my image, it's massacred my grooming. I strive to always look my best, but right now I look my worst, my absolute worst ever. I hate looking like this. Don't I have a handkerchief somewhere? What have I got? Car keys, drugs, silver-plated executive ball-point pen, Leatherman Super Tool, drugs, Nokia picture-phone, drugs, iPod, earbuds, stashbox (full of drugs), some papers ... here's the Google Maps instructions from Anchorage to Noplace. One eight and a half by eleven sheet, white bond inkjet printer paper, folded. Walter, what do you think of this?

A little rough. But it'll do.

Oh yeah. Marcia. Marcia in a halter top. Marcia in a fur thong. Marcia naked on her hands and knees, hair messed up, face in the pillow, hands clutching the carpet, and me behind her pushing my Monster Black Torpedo, laughing, making her take it, and her, whimpering, covered in fur, turning into a bear, growling ... hang on, no, not that. That's too weird.

Back up. Just Marcia now. Yeah, beautiful Marcia. Her hot naked body. Her lurching nipples. Me lying naked on the bearskin rug in the executive lav. Her, turned around and squatting down on my Monster Black Torpedo, bearing down on it slowly. Oh it's big, oh, it hurts, it's too big, she wants to stop but I grab her ass and call her 'ho-bag!' and there's a growl, and the bearskin rug comes alive and bites into her leg as she moans, and the blood, the teeth ... oh, god-dammit!

Bears. No, women! Other women. Lots of women. (Bears.) Tits, big round tits with tanning oil on them. Asses, slapping them. Thighs. (Bears.) Whimpering, gasping vaginas crammed full of Monster

Black … Bears. Bears, bears, bears. Fuck, this is going nowhere. Walter, help me out here. You must know something I don't. When I close my eyes I see Mister Bear in a bikini, Mister Bear on my desk, Mister Bear on the floor of the executive lav on a rug made of … me.

Okay, calming down. Regaining control. So maybe now is not the time. Sorry Walter, you're going back inside. I know you're suffering down there little buddy, but things are tough up here too. Things up here are getting a little bit unreal.

What did I take? What did I neglect to take? Maybe I'm going off my Septihone. It said on the bottle that disorientation may occur. I didn't know they meant sexual orientation. Quit fucking with me, Walter — there is no way I'm having sex with a bear.

8

Bears ate everybody. Bears devoured Edna and Marcia and the members of Image Team. Bears swarmed over the Forest Rangers, ripped them apart like bloody cotton candy, seized their shotguns and marched on Anchorage. Right now they're rising up against mankind, a ferocious bear battalion tottering on their hind legs, chewing a bloody swath through Canada on their way to Washington D.C. to eat the President. Eat the tiny bald humans, they cry. Eat them all! They are crunchy!

That's one explanation, at least. Pardon my mild impatience but whoever hasn't rescued me yet is an asshole. Rescue me, asshole! I'm doing my part, I'm maintaining, I'm keeping my spirits up, I'm keeping my enemy distracted so you can sneak up behind him and blow him away with high-powered hollow-point slugs. Or bring a longbow if you want to do it Nuge-Style, I don't care. But my supplies are running thin here, I'm completely out of Bud and Bud Light, I'm rationing the Diet Pepsi but I think maybe the NutriSweet is interacting badly with my medication. I'm getting the shakes, my legs are sending me way too much e-mail, and I keep seeing bear paws out of the corner of my eyes. My ass has cut off all communication. Bugs are colonizing my pants. Mosquitoes are laying eggs in my nose! Mister Bear himself has been gone all day and is still gone but I can't disabuse myself of the premonition that more and bigger and hungrier bears are out there, nearby, looking for meat.

HELP! Isn't that the basic human instinct? The thing that sets us apart from the bears and the ticks and the fungus and all the other bastard wildlife that's feeding on me? Humans help each other. Humans worry about each other. They don't even do it because they want to, it's a factory built-in, like lust or greed or anti-lock brakes. It's Marketing 101, for Jesus-H-Christ's-sake, the basic manipulation of feeling and behavior. I am missing, they worry, they desire to HELP. Ergo, they are here yet. Only they aren't. And what the fuck is up with that? I mean, if I was a worrier I'd worry, but not being a worrier I'm just sort of confused and pissed off.

If my rescue was an ad campaign it would be bombing, falling out of the sky in flames, crashing like the Chevy Nova in Mexico, and the clients would be screaming and the Veeps would be handing me my ass in an ashtray, and I'd be wringing my hair and wondering, why? And I'd almost certainly be firing someone. Lots of people. In fact, at this point I do believe there will be some firings. As a point of principle there must be, even if they do rescue me, some firings. (And they *will* rescue me, god dammit, or they're going to be doing push-ups in a kiddie pool of deep shit.)

Oh, and did I mention that for the last twenty minutes or so, the normally chatty insects have gone suspiciously silent? The frolicsome squirrels? They fucked off. The twittering Alaskan birds, they have flown, and buried in the exquisite silence, under the deafening drip of my fluid leak, I am hearing off in the brushy distance very occasional bear-moving-around sounds: twigs snapping, undergrowth being crushed, fish being farted. Somewhere off in the Alaskan muck, on the left, someone's looking for a midnight snack.

It's not Mister Bear. Mister Bear is light-footed in the forest; you smell his breath, and then you hear his bronchitis, but never his footsteps. He's not here, in fact he's been gone all morning. Mister Bear, where are you at a time like this? I bet you're balling some she-bear *ho-bag* on a bear waterbed in a sleazy bear motel, while I lie here like a duck stapled to the inside of a barrel. Thanks, M.B. Knew I could count on you.

Did I mention that I hate bears? This is just not fair. Fairness doesn't enter into this. I left a party-pack of tender, crunchy subordinates back at Camp Image Team — the official Alaskan Bear Baiting Station, remember, where the bears are supposed to congregate for meals. It's an all-you-can-eat Homo Sapiens salad bar over there. But oh, no, that's not good enough for the refined tastes of Alaska's hoity-toity bears. Won't Big Brown be disappointed when he finds out I'm the only jerky left. No more Spicy Chorizo, no more Slim Jims, just raw leg of Marv. A Marv Bar. Hey Bears! Are you hungry? Peel open a Starv-Marv!

Maybe if I lie really still and try not to smell like anything, whatever it is won't find me. Probably the wind is blowing in the wrong direction for whatever it is to sniff-o-locate me. Whatever it is, it's making a racket. For all the faults of Nature, I appreciate the quiet. Whatever-it-is does not.

Maybe it's an even larger bear. Or something else large: a moose? A beaver? It would have to be a giant radioactive space beaver. Definitely not a squirrel.

It's something that snaps branches, something that hacks through brush. Something largeish, scaryish. Coming closerish.

Maybe if I piss my pants, the bear will be revolted and go elsewhere … it's coming closer, over on the left. Very close now. I am peeing. I am marking myself with my scent. This Marv is taken, find another one.

With a loud cluster of twig-snaps it enters the clearing. I hear its animal breath, quiet but labored. It sounds winded, tired … running from something? Running from the hunt? Are my useless team members in pursuit of this bear, chasing it through the night with their night-vision goggles? … no, my useless team members don't chase bears through the night, they wait around for bears to show up near lunchtime, the lazy dumbshits. This bear though … or whatever it is … is coming closer, walking on its hind legs, sniffing the air … approaching … it smells me, it knows I'm here.

God dammit! I don't just dislike bears, you know, I HATE them. Hate them hate them hate them! I'm *not* putting up with this! I am losing it, losing my cool. No more mister nice Marv! If that bear gets another step closer I'm going to confront it with a display of strength: a mighty vicious roar, animal to animal. You want a piece of me buddy? You want a piece of me? You're fucking with the wrong Homo, buster. Sapiens, that is.

Enough is enough. Don't come any closer! I mean it! I have had it with you bears! I am through! Finito! Over and out! I will not be intimidated, I will not be frightened and I will sure as hell not be eaten!

Look out! Stand back! I am focusing all my rage, all my anger! I am reaching down deep, deep into the inner Marv, the Ur-Marv, down into the collective might of my warrior ancestors! I am summoning the *Beast*! You want the *Beast*? You want a piece of the *Beast*? One more step and you get the *Beast*! The *Beast* inside Marv! The fire! The ancient anger! It's rising up, through my heart, my lungs, my larynx, my teeth! Here it comes …

"AwooooOOOOOOOOOOOOOO!"

How do you like *that*? That's the motherfucking *Beast*, baby! Think twice before you mess with *that*!

Still think you're tough? Show me what you got … oh please! You call that a roar? You sound like a terrified walrus! Like Edna having a panic attack! Ha ha! Girly bear! Does girly bear want to fuck with the *Beast*? Look out, here it comes again …

"AWOOOOOOOOOOOOOOOOOOOO — "

BOOM!

An explosion! The *Beast* wonders what the fuck is up with that, but the *Beast* doesn't care! The *Beast* is raging! Feel the rage …

"AROOOOOOOOOOOOOOOOOO — "

BOOM!

Another one! Crazy … that must be the sound of the fire within, being unleashed! Wow, the *Beast* is hot tonight!

"Ah-WOOOOWAWAWAWOWOWOWowo — "

Ow! Ouch! Okay, the *Beast* felt that! Right in the hip! That hurt! Dammit! How dare you hurt the *Beast*! Now the *Beast* is really mad —

Aaah! Bright blinding light! No! The *Beast* can't see! The fire inside must really be raging out of control now …

Ohmigod … MARV!

… the rage! The fire …

FRANKIE! FRANKIE! WHERE ARE YOU OMIGOD

71

I SHOT MARV!

    … the anger, the aggrivation …

MARV! MARV! IT'S ME! I'M HERE! IT'S JUST ME!

    … the annoyance, the stupidity, the nagging …

FRANKIE! MARV'S HERE! HE'S UNDER THE CAR! I SHOT HIM!

    … the fat, the ugly, the stupid …

MARVIE!! MARVIE PUDDING?! DON'T DIE! OPEN YOUR EYES!

    Ladies and gentlemen, meet Edna. My cream puff. My sweetness. The fat in my bacon. The bullet in my hip.

    So … I'm rescued. Like that. I realize that I should be excited about this. Of course I'm excited! I'm saved! Saved by … god dammit, why did she shoot me? That is *classic* Edna. And now she's shining a Mag-Light right in my face, and screaming my name over and over. Thanks, that helps. But … it doesn't matter. If Frank's really with her, then I'm really saved.

    Saved! Unless I'm dreaming again. No, please … finally, finally, they're here! Ignore the wife, think about the rescue! Oh, sweet rescue! I'm going to a beautiful hospital, in a city where there are no bears and hardly any trees. A beautiful American hospital where the nurses have tight asses and you're surrounded by expensive machinery that glows and beeps with power, and they never run out of OxySufnix, and animals are not allowed …

    Oh God. Now Edna begins to sob, right on schedule. "Marvie? Oh Pudding … I'm so sorry … don't die … "

    " … Edna … "

    "Marvie! What are you even *doing* down there? You look *wretched*! I thought you were some kind of *wolverine*! Oh honey … does it hurt? You're not trying to fix that car yourself are you?"

"Edna, please … my legs … "

The blinding light diminishes as Edna waves the flashlight in another direction … God, if she would just shut up, everything would be so much more okay again. If she would just be useful, if she would just be quiet —

" … AAAAAAAAH! FRANKIE! OH GOD! HE'S HURT REAL BAD!"

And then the blinding light returns as Edna swings the flashlight back and jiggles it in my face as she hops up and down in a blind panic.

Rescued by Retards: the Marv Pushkin Story. Funny how you can lose touch with how stupid a person is after only a few days. Clearly I'm going to have to do the heavy mental lifting here. But where in foresty-fuck is Baumer … Frank Baumer … *Frankie?* Waitaminute … what is this *Frankie* stuff?

Ah yes: taking his timid time, slowly trudging around the Rover like he's inspecting a prostitute for sores, here comes Frank Baumer in his scruffy hunting boots from Sears and his poorly-fitting outdoor gear. Edna, pouting, hands him the pistol. He bends down on one knee and shows me the clean-shaven blandness of his well-fed face, to once again impress me with his iron grip on the obvious:

"Gosh, Marv, looks like you got yourself good and stuck there." He almost looks like he's suppressing a chuckle, but he wouldn't dare.

I clear my throat, business-style. "So glad you're coming up to speed, Baumer. Now gimme some water! Where the fuck have you been? I've been out here for like three days!"

Edna looks at Baumer sheepishly and says nothing.

Baumer hands me a mostly empty Nalgene bottle of Baumer-scented backwash, which I drink anyway. They are both crouched down beside the Rover, peering under the running board at me, looking oh so laundered and smelling oh so clean. Edna leans an arm on Baumer's shoulder, looking sad and frightened and, even after a hardy weekend in the woods, very fat.

"Well I'm *sorry*, Marv, we didn't *know*. We were back at camp, you know, just relaxing. We thought you went home," says Baumer, trying to look all steely-eyed and faux-outdoorsy. And clean shaven, and not caked with scum. "You're sure lucky we found ya," he says.

"Home? I'm the one who led you pussies out here. I could have died! Look at me! Look at my legs! I need two tourniquets and an ambulance! Stat! While you assholes were picking your noses and playing shuffleboard back at Asshole Camp, I've been locked in hand-to-hand combat with ferocious man-eating bears!"

Baumer and Edna look slightly taken aback.

"Bears, ya say?" says Baumer, talking real slowly, "Well heck, Marv … I mean, sorry, but you spilled bear bait all over yourself right before you stormed off. You oughta know better than to run around in the forest with that stuff on you, I mean … you're asking for trouble, don'tcha think?"

Note to self: Fire Baumer. Ruin career of Baumer. Pour bleach on head of Baumer. Dent Toyota of Baumer. Trample cat of Baumer. Burn down house of Baumer. Inform mother of Baumer: Baumer terminated for unnatural acts with Mouseketeers in company bathroom.

But first things first. "Baumer, here's what you do: take my Leatherman Super Tool and cut the sleeves off your shirt. We'll use them for tourniquets. Edna, you go find that jack over there and give it to Baumer. Get the tourniquets tight around my legs before you start jacking up the car."

Baumer looks strangely uncowed. His gaze and his flashlight both wander down my torso, towards where my legs were just three short days ago.

"I dunno, Marv — "

"No you *don't* know! I know!"

"It's just I don't think — "

"*I* am the one who knows. *I* am the one who thinks. *You* are the one who shuts up. That is the thing *you* get to do, and *also* you get to pull me out from under this car and take me home — *pronto*, as in yesterday! The spare tire is under the floor in the cargo hatch. Don't climb *in* the car, it's sitting on *me*. Just lift it out gently ... would you get *going* for fuck's sake, before Mister Bear gets back. Come on, you guys, show me some hustle here. I'm still in danger, you are too in case you care. We're parked in the Bear Zone!"

Edna and Frank exchange a look, and just like that, they dismiss themselves. "Hey! Where are you going! I'm still talking here! Hell-*lo!* Edna! Baumer! Front and center! Right now!"

Incredible. The fuckers. The fuckers are ignoring me! They're just plain not doing what I tell them to when I tell them to do it! I must be hallucinating. Of all the inappropriate times to mess with the *Beast* ... Frank Baumer, I will fire you and then rehire you so I can fire you again, over and over until you beg me to leave you fired. Edna, you just bought yourself a quarter-pounder of trouble and a side of french-fried hurt. Where's Frink when I need him? That pussy would never dare walk away when I'm talking. That pussy understands teamwork.

But *these* pussies … Edna and Baumer are having some sort of private whispering session a few yards away. All I can see is feet, and all I can hear is little breathy esses and tees, like little kids talking in class. They are standing curiously close together, those two. Is Baumer unable to smell Edna's fetid breath and noxious french purfume? Is Edna not concerned that Baumer might accidentally shoot her in the foot with that flimsy sidearm he's dangling in his hand? What are they talking about? What could be more important right now than getting me rescued?

Oh come on. No way. I didn't just see that. Edna stepping up on her tip-toes and leaning into Baumer? Tell me, did she wipe some kind of turd-stain off his nose? Tell me they didn't just kiss. Jesus. What the *hell* is going on here? *Frankie?*

And look, now here comes innocent little thrice-fired Baumer to talk to me again. Like … like it's a sunny day and unicorns are licking our butts.

"Frank … I'm actually kind of *dying* down here? What's the hold-up?"

"Yeah, you're stuck pretty good there, Marv. We're gunna have to go get some help."

"Help? Frank, for Chrissake, don't get help; *be* help. Jack up the car and I won't be stuck. Change the tire and we're home free! I've still got half a tank of gas. We can be in Anchorage by morning and there's a hospital there, but Frank, there's just not much time. I'm low on everything here, beer, food, blood, I need to get going. Frank, look at me."

Frank Baumer ponders this, but he won't look at me. "It's just, it's … it's not that easy, Marv. Those legs won't get you anywhere, and really I don't think it's safe to move you. You need hospitals and stuff. That's the first thing they tell you about the scene of an accident: don't move people. Edna and I will go for somebody in the morning. You gotta just hang in there, boss."

"The morning! What, after breakfast and coffee and yoga? After your beauty sleep? Go *now* for Christ's sake. Look at me, *Frankie!* I'm meat on the hook here! Could you at least pretend to be concerned?"

"Look! I'm really sorry! We just … we can't drive out at night, Marv. There's parts washed out, there's a lot of off-roading and stuff. In the morning we'll go. You'll be okay, you gotta believe me." And then he reaches under and pats my shoulder like I'm his little Papillon. "Be brave, Marv. Don't worry, you're gunna be fine. Just hang in there, tiger."

I grab his loathsome, condescending sleeve. "Not fine! Worried! Just jack up this car and I will nurse my *own* god damn wounds and drive *myself* the fuck home! This is a Range Rover! It's *guaranteed!*"

"Marv, please!" suggests ever-helpful Edna. "Use your anger tools! You could hurt yourself even worse if you get all worked up!"

"Hurt *myself?* You just shot me!"

"I said I was sorry! Honestly, Marv … you've got to hold on a little longer, Pumpkin. Please … for me?"

"First you shoot me … and now you want to see my *anger tools?*"

And then Frank chuckles. Frank Baumer chuckles. At me. He thinks I'm funny. I consider cutting off one of his fingers. I have a knife. I can still hurt people. He says to me: "Marv, you're talking crazy. Don't try crazy stuff. You're in no shape to drive."

And then … then he reaches across my chest into

my right breast pocket … and pulls out the gleaming fob that holds my Range Rover's ignition keys and door/alarm remote. Just like that. Like he knows which pocket I keep them in. Like he's been watching me. I grab for the keys, for his arm, his coat, anything, but my hands are just like big bunches of bananas hanging off my sleeves. And he says: "Just hunker down and hang in there, Marv. Help is on the way. You're gonna live. You're gonna be fine." And he gets up to walk away, the keys still dangling from his limp, worthless wrist.

"Gimme that! Get back here with that! Those are **mine**! Don't you leave!" He walks over to Edna, and they stand there looking at me from a distance. "Edna! Do *not* leave! Bitch, you had better not leave! Get over here right now and jack up this car!"

"Get a *grip*, Marv! Honestly we're doing the best we can. Why do you have to get all grumpy at a time like this?" Edna sobs pointedly, but she doesn't comply. Why doesn't she *comply?*

"*Baumer!* You are so fired if you don't get back over here right now and get busy with that jack!"

Edna stands up with a meaty, phlegmatic sigh. Now I don't see them, I just hear their heavy footsteps crunching back into the forest, Edna's sobs and labored breathing fade out like a steam train rolling away from the station without me.

"Frank! Edna! I need water! I need medicine! Rescue me god-dammit! I'm sorry! I'm bleeding! I didn't mean what I said! I've been under a lot of stress! Come back here and let's just start over. Please! Edna! Did you hear that? Marv Pushkin is saying please, you know I never say please but I'm saying it. I'm asking nicely for fuck's sake, so will you get the fuck back here, I love you already!

Baby! Sugar bumps! I love you, Edna! I'm going to die! If you leave, I'll die! I'll do it, I swear! Edna!"

Silence. Severe silence. It's never this quiet. I'm totally alone. And I'm crying. Like a woman, like a fag, I'm crying.

Note to self: Kill, kill, kill my darling Edna.

HELP! A Bear is Eating Me!

9

But wasn't that the whole point? Isn't that why I brought her along? To get her off my balance sheets, wash her out of my collar, pluck her like the nostril-hair she is?

Certainly not! Oh no, officer, such an unspeakable act never crossed my mind. Kill my own wife? My loveypants, my cream and sugar, my honeydew melon, my ice cream headache? Oh no.

Rather, I thought I'd delegate. Alaska is wild and dangerous — as we've seen — and there's no shortage of mortal threats to which to delegate the wife-disposal chores with which modern advertising executives are so overburdened. People die out here constantly, especially weak, foolish, incompetent, ugly people like Edna. They drown in poorly-marked bodies of water with no lifeguards presiding. They fall off cliffs, into ravines. They are devoured by bears, or trampled by moose, or skeletonized by ticks. And when all else fails, there are always the tragic hunting accidents. In fact, just before we left I bought Edna a brown fur coat with a matching fur hat from Saks. From a distance she made a fine grizzly … but the stupid bitch refuses to wear it.

"It makes me look fat," she said.

"Baby," I enthused, "that coat makes you look fabulous. Being *fat* makes you look fat."

And oh, she cried about that one. She's a prize weeper, Edna is, a real lawn-sprinkler when she wants to be. No sense of humor, and no sense of taste, or of tact, and absolutely zero sense of when to shut up. Excellent sense of whining, though. One of the great whiners of our times.

Mister Bear, you got the wrong guy. You're supposed to be eating Edna, not me. I, not you or Edna, am supposed to be boffing my secret fuck in the woods behind Camp Image Team. But Edna has this incredible talent for fucking me up.

I recall we were enjoying a very late breakfast back at Camp Image Team, Frink and Halsey had finally coaxed enough heat out of Frink's anemic Coleman stove to sort of mildly cook some bacon and eggs. Just to accomplish that had taken them hours, while the rest of us stalked around like hungry snakes, smoking cigarettes and drinking cold, gritty coffee and cleaning rifles and suiting up for some serious killage. I hadn't had nearly enough sleep, for the same reason that Marcia from Product Dialogue was still asleep in her one-bimbo pup tent — because between the hours of 3 and 3:45 A.M. I had traded Edna's toilet-flushing snore for Marcia's pork-holstering fanny in that same single-bimbo housing unit. So I could hardly complain, really, about the loss of sleep. But the absence of breakfast had me murderous.

Edna had risen earliest of all, and there she sat on the self-inflating couch, picking fussily with her plastic fork at the runny eggs on her styrofoam plate, taking issue with Halsey's cooking and the little black bits of flaked-off frying pan, being impossible to please, being difficult, being Edna. Much to my dismay she wore not the brown fur coat but one of those bright orange don't-shoot-me-I'm-not-a-bear hunting vests, over a dumpy blue down ski jacket. Edna doesn't even *try* to look her best.

But I was prepared to accessorize her with a special cologne: Ranger Steve's Sure-Draw Bear Bait, Yukon Formula. The efficacy of Ranger Steve's secret recipe is sworn to on his website by a throng of experienced bear hunters, including celebrity outdoor hunting guide Rock Majestic. (I wasn't able to find a bear bait endorsed by Ted Nugent.) Supposedly Ranger Steve's bear bait is carefully pH balanced to smell exactly like both a honey-dipped pig on fire and a barn full of bears in heat. Supposedly bears swarm to it like flies to shit. Supposedly you just spray it on some jelly donuts, leave them lying out in a spot that's easy to shoot at, the bears show up looking for the party, you blow away the bears. Ad infinitum. With this stuff one could bag a six-pack of bears in an afternoon, if one could just work out how to lash them to Baumer's Toyota. (No bear marks on my Rover, please.)

I loosened the top of the plastic squirt bottle so the juice would spill more easily — it stank badly of bacon fat and cold tuna — and then I considered the choreography. Come from the left? From the right? Throw it at her from here, or sneak up from behind? The thing is, it had to look right because everyone was watching. It had to look accidental. And I'm a direct-approach guy, so I decided I'd just sit down beside her and ... whoops! Clumsy me! Yeah. Perfect.

I took my plate of half-cooked food in my right hand and the bottle of bear bait in my left, walked over to the bouncy, boneless, unpredictably flaccid self-inflating couch where Edna sat, and plopped down suddenly, right up friendly next to my darling wife. And ... whoops!

Clumsy me!

Only my darling stupid wife chose that very stupid instant to jump up, leaving the couch jiggling like a hot water bottle, causing me to lose slightly more of my balance than I had planned to lose, spilling the Ranger Steve's not on my darling stupid cunt wife but on the spot where she had just sat, and then causing me to roll sideways over into that very same puddle of stinking Sure-Draw bear slime.

"Marv! Don't sneak up on me like that! Look what you did!"

"It's nothing, baby, everything's fine. Come sit down over here and talk to me."

"What is that you just spilled all over the couch? It *smells*."

"It's just hot sauce, baby. Try some, it's good on bacon."

"What are you doing? Look, you're ruining your clothes! Didn't you just buy those pants?"

"Oh, c'mon, give me a hug."

"MARV! Are you *drunk*! You smell like dead fish!"

"It's just nature, baby. Nature smells crazy sometimes."

So it goes. Take a gorgeous, majestic, nature-type setting. Add a lovely morning, coffee and a good breakfast. Then apply one fresh Edna, and observe her power to convert it all to crap. Suddenly, everything was going wrong, wrong, wrong. She told me to get cleaned up, and I told her to shut her trap, and she told me not to speak to her that way in front of people, and I told her to seriously shut her trap or experience later regret, and I tried to peel my sticky self up off the self-inflating couch but it stuck to my ass like toilet paper. But wait, there's more: I stepped on a styrofoam plate of lukewarm breakfast that Edna — on purpose? or through her usual incompetence? what's the difference? — left lying on the ground by my foot. And I slipped, fell back on the couch, and got Ranger Steve's on my shirt collar and the back of my neck and all over my camel hair hunting jacket and even in my hair. While all around us like dumb chickens the members of Image Team stared, unblinking, not laughing only because they wouldn't fucking dare.

"Edna, get over here and sit down right now."

"Marv, I think you're having an *episode!* I'm not getting near you *or* that mess! Go clean off, or roll in the mud or something."

And it was just then that Marcia from Product Dialogue popped her morning-coiffed, moisturizer-faced, doe-eyed head out of her pup tent to say good morning to the world. Myself and Ranger Steve were the first men she beheld when she opened her senses to the morning. And like the eloquent spokesperson for Image Team that she is, she emitted the following brilliant line of product dialogue:

"Eeeeeeew! Marv, did something make a poo on you?"

And that set them all off. It was really funny. Baumer held his nose and fanned the air around his face with his hand. "Eeeeeeew!" Frink pointed his egg-caked spatula at me. "Eeeeeeew!" Halsey and Smith and all the others, pointing and pinching their noses and waving at the air like they were trapped in a closet with God's Own Fart. "Eeeeeew!" Oh yes, I was really funny. Had it been Edna covered in stinking slime, I suppose I would have laughed as well. But I was not the audience, I was the joke.

I told them to shut up, and they didn't. I told them

that was enough and it wasn't. I told them they were all fired and they didn't care. So I assigned them all the task of going and fucking themselves with fishing rods. And I climbed in my Rover, put on that Damn Yankees CD and just drove away.

I was leaving, too. I was headed home to my luxury condominium in Seattle. Those clucking chickens could fend for themselves. Without me, they were bear bait on a stick. As far as I could tell, not one of them had brought a gun big enough to kill a bear with, not the big bears that were certain to convene on them when they smelled magic bear hot sauce all over the self-inflating couch. Frink and Baumer were used to shooting ducks and fish. I doubt any of the others had ever hunted a damn thing, and they had all done zero bear research. Baumer was toting a pistol, for Christ's sake. The Alaskan old timers on AlaskanOldTimers.net recommend that if you carry a pistol for protection from bears, you should file the front sight off the barrel, so it doesn't rip your sphincter when the bear shoves it up your ass. Pistols are only good for killing people.

And now, as I sit here pondering this new injury and this latest insult, now I wonder … and now I know. Baumer. *Frankie.* Frank Baumer never had an original idea in his life. He's always stealing mine. Now he's stolen this one. He's not summoning any HELP for me, oh no. He's not going to tell the others that he found me here, and he's not going to summon Search & Rescue. He and Edna will leave me out here to die. Baumer, my oedipal lackey, wants me dead so he can set about worming his way into my position at Wilson & Saunders, moving into *my* luxury condominium with *my* ugly wife, and commuting from there to the Merch building in *my* Rover!

Baumer, you really want Edna? Why didn't you just text me? I'm done with Edna. I'd say you can keep Edna except that for certain complex tax and financial reasons, I really do need her to actually die. But for the weekend, sure, why not? What's a little Edna between co-workers. If you get off humping a splintery knothole like Edna, I say climb on in there.

And my job? You want that too? You think it's easy delegating to a brainless clutch of ostriches? Go ahead and try, see how long you can handle it. The Ups and the Veeps are tough birds, Baumer, who feast upon the failures of underlings. They'll eat you for a taco salad. But please, give it your best shot. I could use a little sabbatical. Take my desk for a week or two and consider it a perk, a little reward for the initiative you've shown this weekend, in so cleverly and ingeniously plotting to kill me. I have to admire your gumption there, your self-startedness.

But the thing is, *Frankie*, when you took my Rover keys you crossed the line. It's the line that separates the people I'm going to kill from the people I'm just going to scream at. I've been screaming and threatening and intimidating the members of Image Team for so long, I think maybe some of you have begun to suspect I'm all bluster and no bite. I certainly haven't bitten any of you recently. I've been lax, Frank, you're right there. I've clearly let my domination of Image Team slip a little. I, Marv Pushkin, am man enough to admit a minor failing of mine. Forgive me, team; I've been under a lot of stress. Keeping you worms under my heel is a tough, thankless task, but it's my job, and if I don't do my job well I can't expect you to do you jobs well.

Therefore: Members of Image Team, by way of

apology for my recent poor performance I am going to shoot Frank Baumer in the face, and Edna in the back of the head, and together we will skin and clean and eat them, to build team spirit. And we will tan their pelts and hang them in the executive lav, where a little backsplash from the executive urinal will only help to reinforce the message I'm trying to communicate.

And what of Mister Bear? I haven't seen him in ages. Moved on to the next injured hunter? Died of wounds sustained while defending my snacks? Shacked up with Mama Bear in a trailer by the stream? I don't know, and I couldn't give an intercontinental ballistic fuck. I'm not angry with you any more, Mister Bear. You're just a pawn in Frank Baumer's evil game.

I'm still going to kill you, though. It's only fair. Please understand that when I kill you, it's not out of malice, but for the urgency of Justice. Because I am the favorite son of the universe, and when I am wronged it must be made right, and that job falls to me because I'm the only man in this god damn forest who's got a clue about anything. Because I'm Marv Pushkin. I am judge and jury and search and rescue. I am ranger and sheriff and hangman and chef. I will get free, and I will get that shotgun, and I will have hot and cold running vengeance installed out here by this time tomorrow. The universe loves me, I always get my way, things like this simply do not happen to me. This is just a sick, demented aberration of the laws of nature, physics and the United States, and it WILL END because I will MAKE IT END because I'M MARV PUSHKIN!

10

Morning of the fourth day. This place is cold, damp, smelly and utterly inconvenient. Stuck under a car, bear ate my feet, wife treacherous, bugs biting, hip wound seeping, blah blah blah. I'm not a complainer, so enough about all that. Here's at least one piece of good news: I finally found a use for the saw blade in my Leatherman Super Tool. It's the one blade I never use, and I've always wondered if maybe it's overkill, maybe I should have bought the smaller version, but now I know I was right to buy the biggest, most modern and most favorably reviewed pocket multi-tool on the market, because I'm going to need that saw blade to saw my own legs off. Try that with the Gerber Evolution.

A bold move, for sure. Drastic? Definitely. But I just don't see any other way out of this pinned-under-car situation. The only HELP out here is self-HELP. All of those management guru books in the executive lav emphasize that a good manager must never be afraid to take strong measures when they're called for. It takes bravery, sure, it takes guts, and it'll take a couple of tourniquets. I'll wriggle out of this jacket and rip off the sleeves of my Ralph Lauren flannel-cotton outdoorsman shirt, sure, why not, I've ruined every other garment I'm

wearing. I'll tie off the tourniquets good and tight, saw
through the legs … it sucks, but there just is no other way.
Saw the bastards right off, and they damn well better have
a human leg donor fresh off the basketball court, knocked
out cold and waiting on the table when I pull into the
Anchorage 24-hour Neurosurgery Clinic. Somebody tall,
with big feet.

Once I saw myself free I'll crawl as best I can under
the car to the front bumper undercarriage, where I keep a
hidden spare key in a little magnetic box. Oh yes … did I
mention that I am *prepared*? Then I'll crawl out and around
to the drivers' side door and haul myself in. Then I will
turn on the electric seat warmers and reward myself for my
excellent bravery and fine guts by eating the Cliff Bar that
waits for me on the dashboard, and maybe snorting some
of the crystal meth that's in the glovebox. Just to stay sharp.
If I can just get in the car, get the gun, then I know I'll
make it. Once I've got the gun. Edna, Baumer and Mister
Bear will get theirs, by shotgun or by steel belted radial.

Shit. I'm going to have to change the tire as well.
But I can do that. Marv Pushkin can do it. Marv Pushkin
can do anything, because the universe loves Marv Pushkin.
I always win. But it's going to be hard. I'm going to need
a superhuman dose of drugs. I've got three OxySufnix left
and four or five other pills, I really couldn't tell you what
they are but I'm sure they're good or I wouldn't have paid
that spotty-faced Canadian air guitarist fifty American
dollars for them in that alleyway in Vancouver. Here goes,
I'm taking them all right now and washing them down with
my very last swig of Diet Pepsi. I'll give them an hour or so
to kick in, and then: Marv Gets Busy.

Morning of the fourth day. Image Team is striking
camp about now, scraping egg off the Coleman stove,

scattering the beer cans and de-boning the tents, setting fire to the inflatable couch. If Frank and Edna walked here from there, how far could it be? A mile? No more than two. Will they pass this way on their drive home?

Home. When I close my eyes I see the road to freedom, the highway out to Anchorage, the pancake houses and bait shops, the trees and gravel and buckling asphalt. The mile signs speed past and shrink down the horizon in the rear view mirror like shit down a toilet. Get me to the ferry building, put me on the gigantic man-made steel boat and motor me away from this medieval third-world state. I want to hear those ferry engines roar, I want to see them frappé the ocean, chopping up sea life with their man-made splendor, I want to sit in the snack bar and watch the coastline glide away from me while I enjoy crisp, salty Lay's potato chips from a foil-impregnated disposable plastic pouch covered with beautiful, seductive advertisements. I want to eat the kind of pre-hunted, pre-killed, pre-skinned, pre-cooked, non-dangerous food that won't become stale or lose crispiness or bite off your legs. The bag shall be covered with joyous paeans to the remarkable flavors and textures within, serving to heighten the exquisite experience of consumption. A list of the chemical additives, a splendid display of UPC zebra stripes, and a website address will also be provided, so that if necessary my Lay's potato chips may provide hours of reading pleasure. I will eat, savor, enjoy and consume every last crispy yellow divot of potato, save for a few greasy crumbs at the very bottom of the bag which I won't bother to eat because I'm *rich*! Rich enough to buy another sack, ten sacks, every sack of potato chips on the boat! I could eat potato chips every day for breakfast lunch and dinner and it would never put a dent in Northwest Chemical Bank's constantly escalating numeric representation of my societal worth. And when I've finished savoring those delicious, frivolously cheap potato chips I will bundle up the non-biodegradable plastic and foil sack into a little ball, walk or crawl or slither to the side railing of the ferry boat, and hurl my litter at the nearest whale, who I hope will choke on it.

Nature is a thorn in humanity's side. Nature's time has come and passed, and I fucking hate nature. Hate it hate it hate it. When I get home, I'm going to eliminate all nature from my life, starting with Wagner.

America almost had nature beat back in the fifties, but then those whale-hugging longhairs worked their way into the infrastructure of society and ate away at our resolve. They declared a cease-fire with Nature, but Nature doesn't know when to quit. Nature keeps spoiling for another fight, and I swear on the dashboard of my Rover that Nature is going to get one from me. I am Homo Sapiens, a Human, and Humans run this planet. Nature is our servant and Nature is our sandwich. Nature could supply us with fresh King Crab, wild Chinook salmon and exotic hardwoods for our mini-bars, and Nature could be satisfied with that, but no, Nature won't learn its place. Nature has to get uppity. So I say: Nature, you are fired.

Alaska, your yard is a mess and the neighbors are concerned. Your excessive sprawl of unregulated Nature must be mowed and edged. Your woods are training camps for terrorist bears; we must log them. Your tundra is full of dangerous road hazards: we must flatten, grade and pave it. Your oil and natural gas reserves might explode at any moment; it is urgent that we drain them. You need cell phone towers and 24-hour convenience stores and freeways full of cops. You need highways and condominiums and billboards, lots of billboards. You need goods and services, DMX radio and Direct TV. You need wireless Internet access in your cars. Only then will America be safe from the natural threat.

You'll thank us later, Alaska. Look at the squalor you live in, your rotting little cabins, your mosquitoes and mud everywhere. Nature victimizes innocent Alaskans every day and you just put up with it. You deserve more, Alaska. One fine day you will go to work in modern, well-lit telemarketing centers instead of dingy dangerous fishing boats. Someday you will meet your deaths in bright clean traffic calamities instead of dirty dark forests like this one.

My brother Jimmy died in traffic. Mom was at work and Jimmy came home after school and I guess he was hungry, apparently he ate something he found under the sink, he thought it was Tang but it was more like Drano. He couldn't breathe, he was choking, drooling blood according to the testimony from the driver of the truck that hit him when he ran out of the apartment and into the expressway. I guess he thought someone would pull over and help him.

But I didn't get those details until years after the funeral. The first I heard about Jimmy's demise was Dad screaming and wailing and shattering the cordless phone against the wall and stomping on the plastic pieces. Then he called me downstairs and made me sit on the sofa so he could tell me something: that Jimmy's not coming next week, Jimmy's never coming, Jimmy's never doing anything any more because of my stupid mother. And then he turned away from me and squeezed his face with his hands, and then when I spoke he turned back and slapped me open handed across the mouth, and then he ran downstairs to the TV room, where he was never to be disturbed, and reclined on his reclining TV seat and whimpered. From down below me he yelled me the news through the heating ducts: Jimmy's Dead.

Jimmy was only five and I was only six, and as I understood Death, it only happened to old people, sick people and animals in slaughterhouses. Unless someone shoots you with a gun. So I wondered who had shot Jimmy with a gun? It must have been Mom, because that's what Dad said. Boy, I thought, Jimmy must have been very, very naughty for Mom to shoot him. And if Mom would shoot Jimmy, would Dad shoot me to get even? Getting even with Mom was all he talked about back then.

I started to wonder when Dad would get around to shooting me. As we rented our clothes for the funeral I thought he'd shoot me because I buttoned my shirt wrong and couldn't figure out how to fix it. On the drive to the funeral I thought he'd shoot me when the car started making an unfixable noise. On the drive home from the funeral I was sure he was going to shoot me soon, because he kept talking about how brave you have to be to get along in the world all by yourself, with no family. Somehow I thought he was talking about himself getting along without me, not vise versa. I didn't know what suicide was. But the following week at school I was called to the nurse's office and Mom was waiting there, looking eternally tired. She made me sit down on the school psychologist's sofa and explained to me that now I was the Last of the Pushkins.

If you weren't so god-damned imaginary you might be wondering why I'm telling you all this. Here's why: when I found out that Dad had died and I would live, I decided right there and then I would never allow anyone to shoot me, nor would I die for any other reason. Other people could go ahead and die if they wanted, but that was not for me. I wouldn't die or lose or be told no, I would have it all my way every day. Other people could suffer, other people could starve or have accidents or get cancer, but not me. And I would take care of myself, because my parents obviously couldn't be trusted. I would put myself first, for my own safety.

I was born anew that day, the day I made that decision. And it's a strange, beautiful joke of human nature how, once you decide that you are worth a little more than other people, you start to meet other people who think they are worth a little bit less than you. The more you take care of yourself, the more others want to take care of you. Not all the people, but enough of them. The road to the top is paved with other people's smiling faces, and those people, by and large, volunteer their faces to be stepped on. It's a funny fact of life. Knowing that, I've climbed, and I'll keep climbing. I'm climbing over Edna and Baumer and Image Team, I'm pulling myself from the twisted wreckage of this weekend and I'm not slowing down. I will not die. I will not lose. I will not starve or go mad or have accidents. I'm doing everything right from now on. I am going to win. I will return to Wilson & Saunders with the bloody trophies in hand, and ascend, Christ-like, to the gilded halls of the top floor.

I'm tired, though. I need to take a little nap, while I'm waiting for the drugs to come on. Rest up for the action.

HUNTER AMPUTATES OWN LEGS TO ESCAPE MARAUDING BEAR. My god, the film rights will be huge. Brad Pitt can play me. John Goodman can play Edna.

Very tired. Nice to finally get tired. Quick nap. William H. Macy as Mister Bear. Or they can use computer graphics. Or a trained bear.

Can you believe they train bears? BRAD PITT AND WILLIAM H. MACY DEVOURED IN STUDIO BEAR CATASTROPHE! Hah. That'd be funny.

Bear bad. Sleep good.

11

Then, like a dream soft and moist, Marcia from Product Dialogue comes to me, squeezing in under the car to warm me with her hot, needy body. She has on the fur coat and hat I bought for Edna, and nothing underneath. She climbs on top of me, pushing me into the mud, she pulls apart her coat and crushes her twin pleasure zeppelins in my cold stubbly face. She's hungry. She rubs up and down against me like a cat, lubricating her crotch with the dark brown Ranger Steve's Bear Bait on my pants and coat. Her eyes are closed, her mouth open in an O, her tongue protrudes slightly as she sniffs my neck, my face, my hair. Now she rips asunder the buttons on my Ralph Lauren flannel-cotton outdoorsman shirt, scraping my chest with her long nails. Now she is biting my ear. Biting it hard. Oh shit, Marcia from Product Dialogue just bit my ear off. She raises her head above me and the bloody ear drips in my eye. Oh baby! I am hard like a two by four. She grinds her hot sex taco against my tweed hunting crotch, clawing at the reinforced zipper, shredding the tweed, freeing my mighty Monster Black Torpedo which springs up and slaps her in the face. Her eyes grow large with addicted need as she begins to lick the juice from its massive brown tip. She stretches her jaw out wide like a snake to fill her mouth with my cock, and bites down hard, gnawing on my big Slim Jim like a Papillon gnaws on a tennis ball. She rips off a few inches, chews heartily and swallows.

"Spicy Chorizo ... oh yeah!" she moans, taking another bite. I feel no pain, only sex, only unbridled animal lust. Her bait-greased nipples slide up and down the shaft of my abbreviated but still astonishingly huge member, and I know very soon I'm going to ejaculate several pints of blood in her face. "Take off the coat, baby," I moan. "It's impossible to get that stuff cleaned." But now the fur is her and she is the fur, it grows from her nipples and her belly and her face. "Do you like it, Marv? I took the hormones just like you said." She licks my face with her long ursine tongue and howls as she mounts my love-jerky. Her fur is thick and soft as ermine and she radiates heat. "Baby I've been so cold," I tell her, "what took you so long?" She growls playfully and bites off my nose.

The grinding, the slashing, the pulverizing accelerates but just before I can release what few fluids remain within me, the Rover's engine turns over and roars to life. Slowly it drives off of us. I look down at my mangled, missing legs, but all I see is fur. I wiggle my toe and a fuzzy paw answers me. I have bear legs now, and bear feet — negro bear feet! Oh shit, this is just too strange. I stand up, waving my hands and sniffing the air. I can walk! It's a miracle! Negro bear feet will do for now, I'll have to get them changed later though.

I feel a strange craving for nuts and berries, but first things first. My Rover accelerates away into the brush. I sprint after it, bear-quick, faster than Jesse Owens, Michael Jordan and Colin Powell combined. I leap onto the roof of the Rover and peer over the rack into the windshield.

Inside, no surprise, it's treacherous Frankie Baumer and aggravating Edna … but what's this? Baumer is wearing my camel hair hunting jacket and my driving glasses, and on his cuffs are my M.L.O.T.P. cufflinks! And Edna wears Marcia's camo halter top and headband, and a thick crust of Marcia's makeup. And her god-damn Papillon dog Wagner is on her lap, gnawing on the Oxford leather armrest and scratching flea eggs onto everyplace. Edna studies the map in her right hand, while with her left hand she massages the inside of Baumer's pathetic thigh. I choke back the urge to vomit; mustn't ruin the paint.

And what's that behind them, piled high in the cargo area and the folded forward back seats? Piles of multicolored fur, some claws, some heads, all sticky with gore. It's a big pile of dead bloody bears, brown and black. On the top of the pile is a baby black bear no larger than a two-year-old child, its small innocent bear face twisted into a death-snarl of agony. It wears leather motorcycle clothes and cracked reflective sunglasses. It's Bomber. Baumer killed Bomber!

Clutching the roof rack with my hands, I smash my bionic bear feet through the windshield. Edna and Frank scream as the car spins out of control, slides off the road and comes to a precarious stop on the edge of a steep ravine. Frank jumps out of the car wielding a shotgun, but I'm faster. Before he can aim I leap, somersault and land on him, slashing his face off with my bear claws. "You killed Bomber!" I scream. He shoots wild, unable to see, but then I am upon him, biting his hands — he's even got my fucking Rolex! — until he drops the gun. I drag him to the car, remove his suede chukka boot and begin to eat his delicious almond-scented foot.

But then out of the car leaps Wagner, grown

now to the size of a huge husky, clutching the chewed up, slobbered-upon, tooth-perforated remains of my Rover's passenger right-hand armrest in his mouth. Fucking dog! I run to kick him but he leaps up and locks his jaw onto my arm, simultaneously wagging his tail and blinking at me with those cute puppy dog eyes. I hate that! I gouge his eye with my other thumb and he yelps.

Edna, standing beside us, complains: "Marv, be gentle with Wagner! He's just playing." Now blood streams from my forearm as Wagner scurries behind Edna's feet, chewing innocently on the passenger-side airbag.

"You stupid cow! You useless bag of tits!" I scream. "Your damn dog ate my car! Your damn boyfriend killed my bear! All you do is ruin everything! With your complaining and your condescending, your whining and your tittering, and your not ever dying!"

Edna looks sad and regretful. Wagner, too, is curled up on the ground with his paw over his nose, avoiding my gaze. "Oh Marv," she sobs, "I'm sorry, Sweet-ums."

"You ought to be sorry! You were supposed to die years ago! You have a congenital heart defect! I wouldn't have married you if I thought you'd live so goddamn long!"

"I didn't mean to ruin your weekend, honey."

"Well you did a bang-up job, I gotta say. Spilling bear bait all over me, shooting me in the hip, not dying ... *Frankie* ... how do you do it? What's your secret?"

"I'll just die now," sniffles Edna contritely.

"Oh I *wish*. That's what you always say."

"You're going to have to learn to take care of yourself sooner or later, Marv."

"Oh please. You sound like Dad now."

"Sorry, pudding. Okay, I'm dying. Bye." And then she dies — just falls over like a bag of groceries, lands face flat in the mud. Wagner whimpers and licks her, but she doesn't move. She's dead.

Wow. That was easy. It never occurred to me to just ask. *(Note to self: read up on Power of Asking.)* I look to pick up the shotgun, but it's gone, and Baumer's gone, and now Edna and Wagner are gone too. Good riddance! I walk to the Rover, my ticket to freedom, I put my hand on the drivers' side door latch ... but now I'm really **craving**, actually, some nuts and some berries. I haven't had nuts and berries in weeks. And now that I'm free from the cacophony of stink that I've wallowed in for days, I can actually smell something ever so slightly nutty around here someplace. Mmmmmm. Nuts.

So I follow my nose into the forest, which is just lovely to traverse when you've got bear feet, inside Armani slacks and Prada loafers. Finally, I'm looking my best again. I look fantastic, sexy and clean. And ahead through the boughs of giant cedars and bushes on the forest floor I spy something impossibly beautiful, the glowing sign, the cathedral-like windows, the tiny parking lot: it's a 7-11! I feel tingly all over, and a tear comes to my eye. Convenience, how I missed you!

The electric eye trips the doorbell as I enter and scan the aisles for nuts. What an oasis of beauty! The sounds, the colors, the flavor shapes! The sweet buzzing of the fluorescent lights and the soft, soothing harpsichord and trombone rendition of Wild Thing floating from the overhead Muzak speakers. The hot, tight-breasted babes of the beer and cigarette advertisements, and the cigarettes, and the beer.

The store is crowded with woodland creatures. A pair of jackrabbits have climbed up on the beverage counter to push a Big Gulp cup under the Slurpee dispenser with their heads. Squirrels crawl through the magazine rack. A deer clatters his hooves on the controls of the video game in the corner.

And who would be napping behind the counter but my old friend Mister Bear! Looking sharp in an 4XL polyester 7-ll uniform shirt and matching paper hat! His little employee tag reads: BEAR. I'm proud of you, Mister Bear. You have embraced consumer culture, you'll have no trouble adapting to the Alaskan de-naturalization program. Bears are resilient creatures indeed.

My saliva draws me to the brightly lit Nut and Berry display. Roasted macadamias! I'm so hungry. I grab every nut on the rack. Each nut is individually wrapped with a serving suggestion and UPC code. I pile the nuts on the counter, along with a 40 ounce bottle of berry-flavored malt liquor, a pack of Camels and a copy of PLAYBEAR. Mister Bear looks up groggily from the floor.

"Hey, Mister Bear! Remember me? It's Marv Pushkin!" But Mister Bear shows no recognition, he just lazily scans each nut one at a time with the paw-held laser UPC scanner and drops them in a plastic bag. Beep. Beep. Beep. This will take forever. Beep. I tap my knuckle on the counter and gaze idly at my left wrist. Beep. One of the nuts won't scan for some reason, and Mister Bear has trouble entering the code number on the ten key pad of his cash register. Beep. He scratches his head and yawns. *(Note to self: don't hire bears.)* I notice on the register that these nuts are not cheap. I reach for my wallet, but my pants are gone. Looking down I see only my underwear and my furry bear legs. Beep. Oh, how awkward. I'll have to hike back to the Rover and dig some cash out of the dashboard mini-safe. But … I'm *so* hungry, and the sweet aroma of the nuts tortures me, so close, so delicious … I've got to have those nuts!

Quick as a subliminal advertisement I snatch the sack of nuts and the 40-ounce bottle off the counter and dash out the door, into the woods. I hear an alarm — Mister Bear must have tripped it — but I sprint with my amazing bear feet, faster than Maurice Green or Mister T., deep into the dark woods, until I can no longer hear the claxon. Then I tear open the bag and stuff the individually wrapped nuts in my mouth, wrappers and all. I chew, chew, chew, they are so delectable! I swallow a little bit of plastic but who cares? In moments I've eaten the last of the nuts and spat the cardboard out of my teeth. I'd like to wash it down with some berry flavored malt liquor but without my Leatherman Super Tool I can't remove the bottle cap. And I'm still hungry. Oh, so very hungry! I wonder if there's a Taco Bell back near the 7-11 ... but no, I can't go back there now.

The forest is my snack bar. Wafting on the breeze I can smell raspberries, almonds, trout, cafe au lait, pizza, everything a person could need is here, somewhere in this forest. I only have to follow my nose. I choose raspberries, and set out to find them.

I'm finding it's easier to master the terrain if I walk on all fours. But as I amble along the forest floor I find a curious swath of broken twigs and crushed vegetation, and at the same time I catch whiffs of both fresh bacon and Marcia from Product Dialogue perfume. Interesting. So I follow this trail a short distance, and ahead of me on one side of the trail I see a black lump. Could that be what I smell? No ...

I get closer and I see an inert pile of black fur and fabric. Oh dear. It's Bomber again. Still dead, lying face down. Only he's not wearing his motorcycle outfit any more, he's wearing a tiny bear version of the polyester print 7-11 shirt that Mister Bear wears at his job, and a matching hat. He's been crushed to death, and a muddy tire print runs down the length of his back. Oh God, this is really sad, this is gross and awful … oh, poor Bomber, don't you know better than to run out in the road?

Now Mister Bear is here beside me, a fat tear forming in the furry corner of his eye. He sniffs the dead bearchild, lays down beside him, puts his face in his paws and whimpers like a sick dog. I cry too. Who wouldn't? Poor Bomber. He was so young, he had so much potential, he could have gone to college or joined a circus or been one of those trained acting bears, or maybe even gotten a job in a zoo. But I look again and that's not Bomber lying flattened in the dirt, it's my little brother Jimmy, with a bottle of Toilet Duck in his hand, flattened by a truck.

"Mister Bear," I scream, shaking my weeping, disconsolate furry sidekick, "Are you going to take this? I'm not going to take this! We've got to find the fuckers who crushed our families! We need to make an example of them! That's what Justice is all about! Are you with me?"

Mister Bear springs up with a mean grunt of determination and sprints off down the path at awesome speed, and I strain to keep up with him. Then he stops: ahead of us in the trees is a lone building, an isolated forest hideaway. Actually it looks a lot like my luxury condominium in Bainbridge, only instead of cedar shingles it's covered in animal hide, and the luxurious front lawn is landscaped with thick fur instead of grass, and the dramatic front-yard Water Feature is now more of a Blood Feature. Parked in the rawhide driveway is a rawhide-paneled Range Rover. Bear and I creep stealthily up the driveway, wary of hunters.

I peer through the rear window of the Rover and see a pile of human carnage in the cargo area — it's Image Team! All of them, all dead. All of them? What about Marcia from Product Dialogue? I don't see her in there, I see Frink and Wollencott and Smith and there's Baumer and Edna too, and a few more unidentified arms and legs but they look pretty male. This is terrible, catastrophic! This blows six different development schedules! The Ups are not going to be happy about their department being all killed like this, right before sweeps week. Maybe I can get some new hires lined up before I get back.

Mister Bear takes the shotgun from the car and creeps silently up the walkway to the open front door. Inside we hear sounds of animals and human screams. We enter stealthily, although I find I have something sticking in my throat.

Christ, it's like a luxury abattoir in here. In the living room there's blood all over everything: the sofa, the walls, the Venetian shag carpet and the doorknobs. The flat-screen LCD cinema display TV on the wall blares a program from the Animal Attack channel: a small foreign man being devoured by geese. In the center of the room is a cloth-draped surgical table with a bright operating lamp hanging overhead, and a small cloth-draped table beside it holding a glinting array of stainless steel knives and saws. The apartment seems deserted … but when I approach the table bears stream into the room from all sides!

There's two polar bears wearing white surgical gowns and masks. A third polar bear pushes a large wheelchair, and in that chair is a huge, legless Grizzly in bandages, hooked up to a beeping life support machine. The bears surround me on all sides, and stare silently at me. They're looking at my legs. I look down and realize I'm not even wearing underpants, and my Monster Black Torpedo is dripping blood on the crimson rug.

The legless bear raises a weak paw at me and growls, "Mine."

I turn to Mister Bear — he rears up on his hind legs and levels the shotgun right at my heart! Why ... you ... bastard! After all we've been through together! He shoves me backwards with the gun and bear claws grip me and throw me on the table. Mister Bear climbs up on my legs and sits on them, pinning me. The other bears hold me down as one of the polar bears takes a huge Leatherman Super Tool from the tray and opens up the bone saw. I try to scream but no sound escapes my lips. No. They are cutting me up, they are killing me, they are driving iron spikes of fire into my body. No, please! Please, please, give me something for the pain! Doctor, please — the pain! I can live without legs but I can't live with this pain. You can take my negro bear feet, you can take my monster black torpedo, but knock me out, block the pain ...

12

Note to self: fucking **yowch!** It hurts, oh yes, it hurts!
Now I remember pain: pain was exactly like this, only not
so painful. Pain, I got your e-mail, I got your fax, I am
not interested! Will you please stop calling me? What is
up with pain? If I'd wanted pain I would have seen an
acupuncturist, not a pharmacist, certainly not a toothless
Canadian hair farmer with a sideline in prescription
pills. That dickhead dealer sold me bogus drugs! Why is
everybody always trying to rip me off? Please, God, get
this painful hunk of luxury off me. Oh God.

No God. There can't be a God. God wouldn't
take a brilliant concept like Homo Sapiens and fuck it up
with Pain. Only Nature would be so retarded, so cruel.

Hello, God? Can you hear me? This is Marv
Pushkin calling. Yes ... *that* Marv Pushkin. And I'm a big
fan of yours as well. So, if you do exist, could you please
consider dropping whatever important bullshit you're
doing and getting your holy kiester down here to rescue
me and my car? Look, whatever you need, I'll take care
of it if you'll just airlift me out of this forest, I'm a wealthy
guy, I'll give money to Mother Theresa, or the Ronald
McDonald house or whatever. Whatever the fuck you
want, penitence or I'll pray or shit I'll go door to door with

the stupid magazines and talk about how you changed my life! I was dying under a car and now I'm out from under a car and not dying, that would be miraculous to me right now and I wouldn't mind lecturing on that, I could use PowerPoint, I've got a real talent with PowerPoint, I'm like a PowerPoet. Owww, just help me get out of here NOW and we'll work out the details back at my office, or shit we can do it at *your* office, on a mountaintop, in a manger, wherever you say, you're the Man, you're in the driver's seat, I'm prepared to be flexible but *please please please.* Look at me, I'm praying here. Marv Pushkin is praying, so make it snappy with the miracles please!

Please!

Please?

Asshole! I *knew* he didn't exist. Oh, my torture has a first name, it's ow ow OW OW OW! I've got hot needles all the way up my spine and I'm freezing and there's a dozen ticks burrowed into various parts of my ass, laying eggs and tending their new lawns of my butt hair. I've got itchy bug bites on my eyeballs, my teeth won't stop twitching, my mouth is dry as a double-absorbent diaper, I'm so thirsty I'd drink gasoline.

Not That I'm Complaining! ASIDE FROM THESE MINOR ISSUES, EVERYTHING IS JUST GREAT!

Except, did I mention the hallucinations? The Rover keeps melting, collapsing, vibrating, turning blue, advancing and receding. In a different time and place I probably could enjoy that, have sex to it, but then I keep seeing things in the corner of my eyes. When I turn to look, well, who knows what I see since I can't even focus my eyes properly but it sort of looks like tiny ground squirrels in hospital scrubs running around with scalpels and saws. I am inclined to doubt that they are real. I mean, of course they're not real. Give me a break, I'm not nuts.

I bet God does exist, and I bet he's a sick sadistic prick who created the world just to have something small and defenseless to poke. Maybe that's why animals eat people and people eat animals, and justice is so fleeting. Maybe God is laughing at me: my suffering, my pain, my "problems." Maybe my reality is God's Reality TV. That would just about explain all this.

Fuck you, God, I'm leaving. I've got to. I've got to do it somehow. I'm getting out of here with as much of me as I can carry. So long God ... hello Leatherman Super Tool! *You* I believe in. *You* are made from only the highest quality hardened stainless steel, using advanced computer aided manufacturing technologies. You never dull, rust or snap. With you I could disassemble a car, or a rifle, or a TV set. Today we will disassemble a Marv. But first, tourniquets. I have already snipped my sleeves, so just a simple tug ... here ... whoops, slippery ... this should just rip right off ... whoops, dammit. Tool, where did you go? Where's my tool? Tool? It was here, I just dropped it, it's got to be here next to me, I can hardly feel anything but it's obvious it's here, where is it? Back off, squirrels! It's mine, where is it? It's here! It's got to be here! WHERE IS MY TOOL?

GOD DAMN ASSHOLE SHITFUCK PIECE OF CUNT WIPING TAIWANESE TECHNOLOGY WHERE THE COCK FUCK DID YOU GO YOU PIECE OF STINKING ASS CRAP GOD DAMMIT I NEED YOU TO SAW OFF MY SHITPIECE MOTHERFUCKING CORNHOLING CUNTWIPING LEGS, OH DAMMIT DAMMIT DAMMIT, OH GOD IT HURTS IT HURTS IT HURTS — ah, here you are.

Sitting on my leg. Now then ...

Now then ... the saw.

Deep breath. The saw. The legs. For instance: the left leg.

How to do this?

Like ... *so?*

Fuck! Shit! Fuck! Shit! Fuckshit. Ow ow ow. Nope! Wrong. Not like that. That's ... that's maybe not going to work. Hell, I didn't think I could *be* any more in pain, let alone any more bleeding. Dammit! I could do this! If it wasn't for the pain, I'd be free! Oh man, oh God, oh Jesus ... this is not as planned.

But what's that sound ... hello! Look who's come to join the party? If it isn't everyone's favorite stinking mammal, Mister Jesus H. Bear, huffing and puffing and ambling home at sunrise like he hasn't been mysteriously absent for the last day and a half.

Where you been, M.B.? Out partying with your bear pals, I suppose. Didn't even have the courtesy to phone home while I was up all night worrying about you. Well, why don't you just fuck off back to wherever you've been pleasuring yourself. I have some important neurosurgical business to attend to and I don't appreciate your snarky back-seat commentary. It takes a light touch, presence of mind, it's a delicate business and you make me nervous when you stare, so please just give me a half-hour of Marv time. Come back later and I'll leave you out some breakfast.

Don't you speak English? Go, A, Way. Shoo! Mush!

Mister Bear, what are you staring at? Nothing to see here, please move along. Sure, I was stare-worthy once, I was something to see, I was Marv Ascendant, not any more.

110

I stink, I'm sick, bloody and bug-bitten. I wouldn't eat me if I was the last piece of meat on earth. I'm dying, and I hurt like bullets. Satisfied?

Mister Alaskan Black Bear, mister Ursus Americanus, I don't even get you. You are supposed to be largely herbivorous. You are supposed to prefer nuts, berries and bugs. Is my name Herb? Do I look nutty to you? Why are you doing this to me, Mister Bear? Why do you hate me? What did I ever do to you?

That was your cub I ran over in the Rover, wasn't it? Can you smell his blood under the front fender? Is that why you're angry? You can tell me.

I'm sorry. Really, I apologize. But that's the law of the jungle, isn't it? Kill and/or be killed, day in, day out. Someone's always killing your children these days. You can't let it get you down. All the other animals in the forest have predators, how would you deserve a free pass?

No … no it's *not* your forest, you don't *own* the forest. We're all co-owners of This Condo Earth and we've got to share. We're all in this together, am I right? Interconnectedness of all living things, et cetera. I'd expect a bear like you to understand new-age granola concepts like that.

Yes, I know you were here first, but we're here now, and we're not going away. People don't go away. Only Nature goes away.

What do you mean? I have *tons* of respect. Tons! I love this place. Humans adore nature, that's why we come out here to hunt. We wouldn't hunt animals we didn't respect, would we?

Oh, look who's calling who stupid. What's your B.A.T. score anyway?

Smelly? Oh, now the pot of bearshit calls the kettle

smelly! Hah! Go sniff yourself in the mirror sometime.

Hey, hey Mister Bear: I think it's great that you've decided, finally, to open up and share your feelings with me but — no, let me finish — but I sure wish you would have brought some of this up before you chewed my fucking legs off. Maybe we could have, you know, torn down the walls between us, had a weep-in, become spirit siblings, all that would be great for a guy who still had some legs. But right now I'm afraid I'm just a little bit low on sympathy for your bear problems. Ow.

Well yeah, I *said* I was sorry. But imagine how I feel! This sucks, this hurts, this is torture! You're actually torturing me.

Yes! OK! Sorry! Sorry sorry sorry! Don't I look sorry? Isn't that good enough for you? It was an accident! I didn't park on top of your son and eat his feet, did I?

Oh *please*. If I taste that bad, why'd you eat so much of me? Hmm? You know, don't bother to answer. Just forget it. I'm sick of talking to you. You don't understand what's going on here. You still think this is the forest primeval and you can slaughter any old hunter who happens along without fear of reprisal. Don't you realize what you've bitten off?

They're going to take you down, Mister Bear. When they find my carcass under this Rover and they realize there's a dangerous man-eater loose out here, a hunt will be called, and the humans will come, hundreds of loud, stinking humans with their guns and their dogs and their helicopters and their gasoline burning vehicles. They will mow you and your family down in just reprisal, and that's not my fault Mister Bear, that's yours. All the other animals have learned not to hassle the Man. You hassled the Man, now the Man's going to hassle you.

Alone? You wish. Loneliness is obsolete. Haven't you heard? Oh but you don't have the Internet up here yet, I keep forgetting. Poor, disadvantaged bear. Let me give you the rundown: basically, we live in a global village now, we can transport anything to anywhere instantly, all life is deeply and magically intertwingled, all places are connected, and so every place on earth is slowly but certainly becoming more like every other place on earth. The deserts will get a bit more foresty and the forests will get a bit more deserty. I'm sure you've noticed how the winters haven't been as cold as they used to be. Thank us later. Likewise, the wilderness will get more highways and the urban centers will get nicer landscaping. The polar bears are swimming south, the koala bears are climbing north. The property developers are beating a path up here to deflower the last virgin stretches of undeveloped property, while lumber and seafood floats away to Japan in crush-proof canisters. That's the power of the global market: if someone in Taiwan wants a bear hide for their executive lav, market forces will suck it toward them with magnetic strength. But don't worry, because Capitalism is a fair God, a good God, it uses its magic power to make everyone rich, perhaps even bears.

Mister Bear, quit crying. This is nothing to be sad about. Change is good. There's a bright, exciting future waiting if you can just get with the program and find a seat on Capitalism's magic bus. Sure, maybe there won't always be a forest here, but on the other hand if you have any more cubs they'll have great new options. They'll be able to travel. If they can learn certain skills they could be pack animals, or golf caddies, or they could guard the estates of the wealthy, or perform in movies, or there's the circus or they could be pets, maybe, if they could be

declawed and detoothed and maybe drugged or something.
Or listen, even better: I bet the U.S. Army could really use
some mean, tough, strong, do-or-die kind of vicious killer
bears like you and your family. Bear Squadron! You could
go to Iran and fight terrorism!

Terrorism? You know, the guys who hate our
freedom?

Wow, you really *don't* get any news up here, do
you? Okay, terrorism is … well, it's hard to explain, but
you'll know it when you see it — when they invade your
homeland and threaten your way of life!

No, no, no. Not me, not us, totally different people.
With turbans, and really long fuzzy beards. If you see
anybody sneaking up here with turbans and beards, you
be sure and eat them right up, okay? Trust me, they're
delicious.

Shit. Mister Bear, I'm sorry things turned out the
way they did. If you could get to know me you'd see I'm
really not a bad guy. I'm sorry about your son, not that it
makes a difference. But I have to ask you a favor, Mister
Bear, because I am going absolutely nuts. From this pain.
I move my eyeball, my thighs throb. Just talking hurts, just
thinking hurts, just living. Everything hurts and all I want
is for it to stop. I've got a low, low threshold of pain. If you
were torturing me for information I would have long ago
told you everything you wanted to know and everything you
never cared about and I'd be making up new exciting facts
just to please you. My brain's boiling, my hair's screaming,
I'm so thirsty and hungry and cold, and I can't make my
hands move, and I just want to die now. All I want is to die
and I can't even do that by myself. That's the favor. Can
you help a brother out?

Look: it's okay if I die. Because I'm going to live

forever. Somebody's going to find me eventually, find this wreck, and they're going to piece it all together, everything that happened to me. My story will live on. Marv Pushkin the man may die, but Marv Pushkin the story, Marv Pushkin the book, the docudrama, the action figure … the world will know. And the world will care, and the world will spend money on that care. They will love me when I'm gone, they'll put fucking statues of me in major metropolitans areas. Marv, Last of the Puskins. Master of Men. Battler of Bears. The Fallen One. The Hero! If they really care, then they'll clone me, yeah, I may die but they'll clone me later. Death is temporary when you're rich, and I'm going to be the richest dead man who ever lived, because I've got the greatest story ever sold! So it's okay. Everything is going to be fine. I just need something for the pain.

Mister Bear, whatever else you may think about Homo Sapiens, know this: when a person sets out to kill a bear they try to do it quickly. We call that Being Humane. Do you grasp the concept? Are you humane, Mister Bear? Can you help out a guy who's farther down on his luck than perhaps any Homo Sapiens has ever been? Please?

If I lean my head out this way, can you reach my neck?

Oh c'mon, please?

What's the matter? Do you hate the sight of blood? Too squeamish to kill a little pink human in cold blood? Are you paralyzed by bear ethics? Come on, kill me! You know I'd do the same for you!

Why … what do you smell?

A sudden loud explosion — fur and bone and brains flung across the clearing — the crackle of a rifle blast echoing off the trees. One side of Mister Bear's face hangs open in dripping, bloody tatters. Hunkered low to the ground, panting and spraying blood. He looks at me through bloody eyes: angry, confused, sad, afraid.

But not dead.

He climbs back on his feet — with an ancient roar of pain, he bounds toward some hidden enemy —

Another explosion! ... he drops again to the ground, shot through the heart.

Growling, crying, choking, he rises again to his feet and faces his executioner. Stands motionless, about to topple, blood streaming from him in puddles on the ground —

Like a buck he springs! Sails through the air in a furious lunge! He screeches —

They shoot him one more time.

He drops. And dies.

Who shoots him? Hello? Who's there? Who shot my bear? Rangers? Hunters?

Grizzlies.

Oh dear. Here they come, a sleuth of them, ambling on all fours, done up in orange vests and porkpie hats. This is weird, this is bad, this is new dimensions in bad weirdness. One grizzly approaches the corpse of Mister Bear and prods it carefully with the shotgun tip. Bears with shotguns. This is very bad, this is a real problem now. Oh hell, they're all over. They've got me.

"Mister Pushkin! Marvin Pushkin! Can you hear my words?"

I'm dead. Go away. I'm not a threat. Look at me, I'm so dead. You never saw such a dead, dead person. I've been dead for ages.

"All right, stretcher over here. He's still breathing. Call in the helivac!"

I'm *not* breathing god dammit, I did not breathe you cheating bear, get your filthy trout-laced paws away! Oh shit, it's bears bears bears. Now they're OW OW OW don't move the Rover! No! Get away! I know Bear Survival Tip Number Three! I've got a Super Tool! Paws off!

"Woah! Mister Pushkin, take it easy! We need to … Sam, we got a non-cooperator here."

Fucking bears! I hate you! I have had it up to here with being pissed on and parked on and snacked on and poked and prodded by bears. You've had all of me you're going to get. You, with the gloves, you want my knife? Here! Ha! The claw's on the other foot now sucker! You think you're *so* smart because you can balance on your hind legs —

"Yowch! Sam, he cut me! Gimme two tourniquets,

stat! And, and six inches of gauze. Shit."

— dress up like Smokey Bear and shoot guns?
Dance on a ball and juggle salmon? You're not fooling
anyone. You think you're going to take over just like that?
Drive our cars —

"Sedative! 300 ccs of Klonopin, in the orange box
with my kit over there … "

— wear our clothes, imitate our voices like big furry
parrots. But that's not what makes a Homo Sapiens, not
even close. Get away!

"Hey Mister Pushkin, it's O.K, calm down, we're
getting you out of here, just … Sam! Hurry up with that
shot!"

I'll fucking cut you! I will, I've got claws, sharp sharp
sharp! Human beings will always beat you because we've
got civilization on our side. Cut one of us down and a
hundred more will spring up in his place. We're organized,
we stick together. We've got the shoulders of giants. You've
got berries and nuts. You're nothing! God made you to be
shot! By us! Get off, off, no! OWW! Fucker! I'll bite you
for that! Let go! Let go of me! Insolent Yogi bath mats!
No!

"Here, pry his fingers. Mister Pushkin, you could *still
die* if you don't quit — "

What's that? Oh Christ no, don't tell me the bears
have a helicopter. It can't be! They've got guns, trucks,
radios, clothes, helicopters too … how long have they been
planning this? Is this war now? The terrorist bear invasion
finally happening? No, it's impossible: bears are stupid.
YOU ARE STUPID. Jesus, look out, it's a chopper full of
bears! They'll crash, they'll explode, they think the joystick
is a Slim Jim! I'm not going up there, it's pure death, no!

"Cinch him up, he's jerking around still. Tell

Evergreen to break out some plasma and keep him strapped. Ugch, that ain't pretty … "

No! No! Let me go! I want my car! I'm dizzy, I'm sick, I'm thirsty, I'm dead, I have botulism! Don't eat me! Oh the sky is too bright and the wind is too loud and the rope is too long, but here comes the chopper, chop chop chopping up Marv Pushkin, to sell my meat on the bear market. Hah! Badda bing! Oh, I crack myself up, I crack up, I'm cracking, I'm going through the windshield with my positive mental airbag, I'm positively fucked, oh please, just cut the rope, cut it, I can't, I'm at the end of it, my rope, ha ha! I'm so funny I'm so finished I'm so fucked, don't you know? Don't you get it? That's the difference, mother-bearfuckers, that's why you'll always lose because a bear couldn't tell a joke to save my life.

13

Forward and back.

Forward and back.

Forward and back.

Forward and back.

Forward and back.

Forward and back.

Forward and back.

Forward and back.

Forward and back.

Forward and back.

Forward and back.

Forward and back.

Forward and back.

Forward and back.

Forward and back.

Forward and back.

Forward and back.

Forward and back.

Forward, back.

Forward, freeze.

Back.

The bear problem … it's out of hand. Way out of hand. They're in the cities, they walk the streets, they drive the cars, they talk on the cell phones. They act like people, and it's funny but I think they think they *are* people. And they think they can fool Marv Pushkin. That's how dumb they are. They think they can skin a human being and wear him like a leisure suit over their flea-bitten bear bodies and I won't notice the difference. But the smell betrays them. I can smell them a mile away.

Forward and back.

This whole zoo reeks of bears. Polar bears push clipboards and carts around the halls all day. Koalas change the sheets. Pandas peer in at me through that mirror on the wall. Oh yeah, nice mirror! You think I've never heard of two-way glass? Bears are so naive.

Forward ... back.

But positivity wins the day. Check out my new ride! The luxury automated 2007 TDX-5 Freedom Throne, by Zipper, with executive option package and motorized tilt. They really call it that, a Freedom Throne. Bear humor. The big, particularly ugly and stupid panda who calls himself my Case Coordinator tried to snowjob me that the Freedom Throne was a gift from Image Team. Like there's still an Image Team, like there's still Ups and Veeps in the Merch building. That'd be nice. No, it's all ursine squalor now: frolicking in the board room, shitting on the floor of the executive lav, chewing on the Aeron chairs, urinating on the PowerPoint projector.

Forward. Back.

Why haven't they eaten me, you ask? Excellent question. Obviously I'm tasty and well-seasoned. Clearly I possess the tangy flavor bears crave. But I think they want something else from me. Information. They lock me up, they ask me questions, they put tranquilizers in my food, and now they give me this Freedom Throne. It's part of some elaborate Good Bear/Bad Bear program they want to run on me.

But we're keeping it positive, right? Chin up! So — check out the option package! Servo-adjustable lumbar support, very nice. Walnut armrests — classy! Integrated Fecal Management downstairs — surprisingly useful. Three wheel independent drive train really grips the linoleum. Watch this:

Forward ... back!

Man, I can do that all day. It's relaxing, it helps me think. In my previous crappy chair my wrists and shoulders would get sore from the leather straps, and I got thumb-blisters. But this chair's got neoprene-coated teflon comfort-restraints — I hardly feel them! And with just a flick of this little force-feedback joystick, I can go anywhere in this eight by ten room.

Forward. Back. So easy.

Well, no, it's no Range Rover ... thanks, I *know* it's no Range Rover. Range Rover doesn't even *offer* Integrated Fecal ... oh just shut up. You don't exist, at *all*. That's what I hate about you. You think I *wouldn't* rather have my Rover back? Plus my feet, my legs, my knees, my Aeron chair, my wide-screen condominium, my luxury department? Fuck you! I'm a prisoner here! I'm just trying to, you know, look on the bright side a little? Maintain a positive mental attitude? A Can-Do attitude? Have you heard of Can-Do? Is fucking-off a thing you Can-Do? Why don't you give it a try? Oh, sorry, I forgot, you can't even fuck off because YOU DON'T EXIST. Boo hoo for you hoo. That's actually fortunate for you, because if you did exist I'd drive right over your asshole foot. I'm not taking any shit from any voices in my head today. I, Marv Pushkin, *do* exist, and soon *I will* fuck off. Far, far off from this place I will fuck. I will escape.

My plan? Nothing, no, not yet, no plan as such. I'm still, you know, feeling out the situation. Exploring the options. I'm keeping them interested; I cooperate but I don't talk. Every day bears come and try to convince me they're not bears. (Not going to happen.) They pretend to be my friends, and insist they want to help me. (Help me down their throats, maybe.) And they keep asking me if I want to go home.

But that's not where I want to go. The bear who ate Edna is waiting for me there.

I've had several visits recently from the bear who

ate Edna, who now wishes to be called Edna and wears Edna's skin like an ill-fitting maternity garment. I am trying to be cordial with this bear, for two reasons. First of all, this bear ate Edna. I appreciate that. It's the only thing that went right on my whole vacation. For that I am grateful. Secondly, this bear seems to call the shots here at the zoo, at least regarding me. For instance: my Case Coordination Panda asked what I wanted to eat on Thanksgiving and I told him: nuts and berries. He really didn't like that. He refused to bring nuts and berries. I'm sure he wanted them all for himself. But when I brought this issue up with The Bear Formerly Know As Edna, she raised a good bear ruckus, growled and snorted at Doc Panda and the nearby polar bears, probably bit somebody, and now, whaddya know! I get nuts and berries every Sunday. Clearly, keeping Edna the Bear fooled is key to my escape plan.

And it's easy. I've got them all eating out of my hand. They think I love them. They think I'm happy in this zoo. I was angry when I got here, I was spitting piss and shitting mayhem, but I'm all smiles now. I look down at the empty space below me and wiggle my invisible toes, I gaze around me at the walls and out the window at the bears driving on the highway and I just smile. Nothing can get me down. I'm Mister Positive. I'm Marv Positively Pushkin.

Forward and back. Effortlessly with the little joystick here. I'm itching to take this thing off road and get some mud on these fenders. See how my throne handles some real freedom. Because clearly the cities are not safe anymore. That's bear territory. When I bust out I'll head north, back into the woods. Somewhere I can hide out, somewhere I can get a clean shot at things moving toward me, someplace quiet where I can use my senses. I could hold out indefinitely up there in Alaska. There's plenty to eat, you just need a good warm coat and sharp claws. I could fashion an S.U.V. out of mud and sticks, and live underneath it.

They have really excellent nuts and berries here, I should mention. Of course you'd expect bears to import only the finest nuts and berries. Last Sunday I had Brazil nuts, lightly roasted and salted, and a bowl of strawberries with whipped cream. The whipped cream didn't do much for me but man, the berries were exquisite. I've started agitating for trout, but Doc Panda doesn't like it. Doc Panda wants all the good food for himself.

Thump thump thump? Speak of the devil! Over the hidden intercom comes a furry imitation of a caring human voice: "Hello Marvin. May I come in?"

Forward and back. Forward and back. I'm really not in the mood, but you have to humor them. The electromagnetic door lock hums and in waltzes my Case Coordination Panda with his clipboard and his turtleneck and his little round bear glasses, trotting up on his hind legs like a pro. From a distance he might look human, but his snout sticks out too far. Look, he's brought a chair, and he sits on it backwards, folding his arms over the back and facing me in this let's-have-a-friendly-but-highly-confrontational-little-chat way of his. Stupid panda can't even sit on a chair right.

Hello doc-tor. How goes the revolution?

"I'm very well, thank you Marvin for asking. And how are you today?"

Forward and back.

"I spoke with your friend Ms. Pennington today. You remember Marcia, don't you? She says she hopes you're feeling better … and she wants you to know that her nose is healing nicely."

Forward. Back. Doc Panda pretends to jot a note on his clipboard, pretends to adjust his glasses. Hah. Doc Panda watched too many doctor movies in bear terrorist training camp. What a ham.

"You know, your friends care about you a great deal, Marvin. Every day they call to ask how you're feeling and what they can do to help. Your wife and your friend Marcia are both very concerned."

I convincingly pretend to appreciate the fake concern of my former dead bear-eaten so-called friends.

"Marvin, why did you bite Marcia?"

Back.

"Marvin, please use your words. Don't growl."

How do I explain this? The bear that ate Marcia walked through the reinforced padded doorway yesterday, wearing the clothes I bought for Marcia and the perfume I bought for Marcia. And in the pumps I bought Marcia this bear's ass was looking fine. I don't know, I was confused. So I made small talk, I laid on the charm. It had been forever since I got some. I asked her to sit on my lap, what was I thinking? She started touching me and sniffing me and then the bear that ate Marcia tried to touch Walter, and I saw its bear teeth and the hunger in its bear eyes and I came to my senses just in time to apply Bear Survival Tip Number Three.

But I can't tell that to a panda. He can't know that I know.

"You're a human being, Marvin. Not a bear. You know that, don't you?"

Forward. Freeze.

"Marvin, any time you feel like talking, I'll be here."

Doc Panda pats my shoulder condescendingly, then whips it away before my teeth can close on his paw. He takes a deep breath, attempts a toothless grin, and the door hums and clicks. Out he waltzes with his little chair. The door clicks shut with the snap of a loud iron mechanism, a piece of technology that bears did not invent and do not deserve. Then through my little food slot is slid a tray full of supper. But I'm really not hungry.

The sun's going down in my little window. The bears on the highway are backed up thick and slow. The leaves are falling from the trees, and out there on the big lawn a pair of koala bears push them into little piles with buzzing gasoline leaf blowers. Stupid bears ate all the Mexicans and now they have to tend their own lawns. They just can't delegate. Stupid bears.

They must have been planning this for years. I'm sure they had secret bases in the woods where they drilled on walking, English, driving, firearms, dressing and undressing, facial expressions … and then they swept down from Alaska and Northern Canada in a wave of carnivorous fury. They wanted what we had, and they took it, and now they have it they're not totally sure how it works.

They can't have gotten it all. They took Seattle. They must have taken Portland, probably they took most of Canada. But what about Texas? Mexico? There's just not enough bears to push that far. Bears hate the desert, they're too furry, they overheat. What about France? China?

Homo Sapiens are still out there, I know it. They have to be. When winter comes and all these bears curl up in their living rooms and hibernate, humans will strike back with a blazing counter-attack. They will take back the cities, one by one, and drive the furry interlopers into the ocean to be devoured by sharks. It will be brutal and cruel, and many will die … but not Marv Pushkin. Homo Sapiens will come back for me, and I'll be safe here until then, biding my time, waiting for rescue. Pretending to cooperate, smiling a lot, keeping my trap shut. I can't let these stupid bears know what I know, or even that I know they're stupid bears. I will never, never, never let them win. No bullshit bears will ever break Marv Pushkin.

Forward and back. Okay, I lied, I'm hungry now. What do we have?

Walnuts and cranberry sauce! Hooray for Sunday.

LaVergne, TN USA
25 February 2010
174175LV00002B/10/P